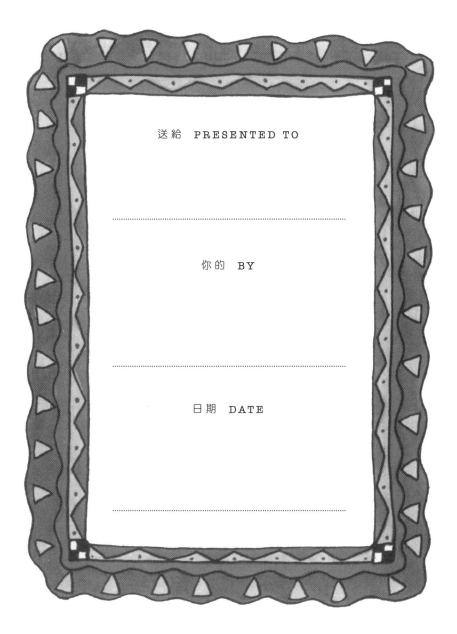

送給 PRESENTED TO

你的 BY

日期 DATE

新編幼兒聖經第二課

原著及出版：Gold 'n' Honey Books, U.S.A.
作者：©V. Gilbert Beers
繪圖：©Terri Steiger
譯者：唐美莉
審閱：周簡艷珍
美術：陳鳳敏
出版及全球發行：純真出版有限公司
香港郵政信箱一〇一二七號
一九九七年九月初版
版權所有　請勿翻印

THE EARLY READER'S BIBLE

The Early Reader's Bible was previously published by Gold and Honey,
a division of Multnomah Publishers

© 1991 by V. Gilbert Beers
Revised edition:© 1995 by V. Gilbert Beers
Illustrations:© 1995 by Terri Steiger

Traditional Chinese Edition:
1997 by Mountainwood Publishing Limited
Translated by Tang Mei-Li

International Standard Book Number: 978-962-8169-02-3
Printed in China

ALL RIGHTS RESERVED
No part of this publication may be reproduced, stored
in a retrieval system, or transmitted, in any form or by
any means - electronic, mechanical, photocopying,
recording, or otherwise — without prior written permission.

For Information:
Mountainwood Publishing Limited
G.P.O. Box 10127 Hong Kong, China

12　13　14　15　16　17　18 — 12　11　10　9　8　7　6

新編

幼兒聖經

第二課

The Early Reader's

Bible

小孩子自己能夠閱讀的聖經

AS TOLD BY **V. Gilbert Beers**

ILLUSTRATIONS BY **Terri Steiger**

純 真 出 版 有 限 公 司

Zonderkidz ™

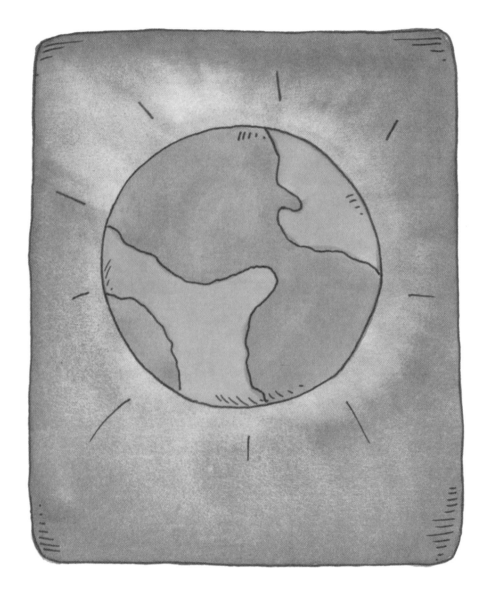

天父創造萬物

創造 · 創世記 1-2

很久以前，世界是不存在的。
沒有太陽，
沒有月亮，
也沒有星星。
天父說：「我要創造一個世界。」
這樣，天父就創造了我們的世界。

God Made
Many Things

Creation · Genesis 1-2

Long ago there was no world.

There was no sun.

There was no moon.

There were no stars.

"I will make a world," God said.

So God made our world.

天父說：「我要造一個太陽。」
這樣，天父便造了太陽。
天父說：「這是個美好的太陽，
它讓你在白天可以看見。」
天父說：「現在，我要造一個月亮
和很多的星星。」
跟著，天父造了月亮和星星。
祂說：「它們是美好的，
你在晚上也可以看見了。」

"I will make a sun," God said.
So God made the sun.
Then God said, "It is a good sun.
It helps you see all day long."
"Now I will make a moon," God said.
"And I will make stars."
So God made the moon and the stars.
"They are good," said God.
"They help you see at night."

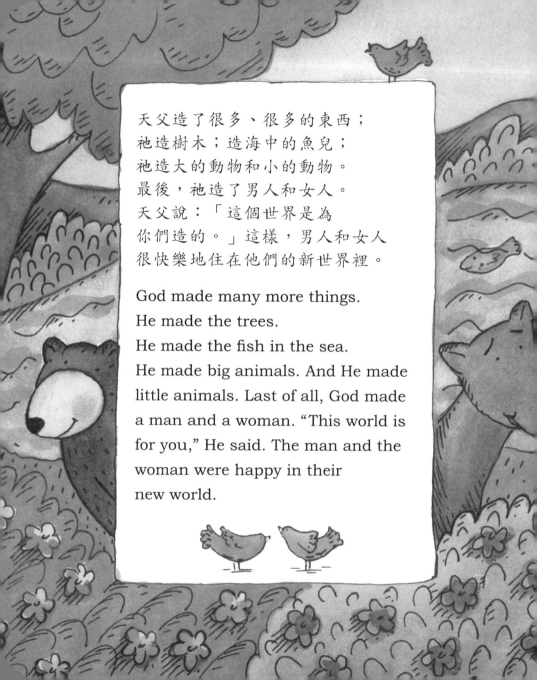

天父造了很多、很多的東西；
祂造樹木；造海中的魚兒；
祂造大的動物和小的動物。
最後，祂造了男人和女人。
天父說：「這個世界是為
你們造的。」這樣，男人和女人
很快樂地住在他們的新世界裡。

God made many more things.
He made the trees.
He made the fish in the sea.
He made big animals. And He made
little animals. Last of all, God made
a man and a woman. "This world is
for you," He said. The man and the
woman were happy in their
new world.

問答題 Something to Ask

1. 誰創造了這個世界?

2. 誰造了太陽、月亮和星星?

3. 誰創造了所有的動物?

4. 你喜歡天父創造了所有的東西嗎?

5. 你有沒有感謝祂?

1. Who made the world?

2. Who made the sun, moon, and stars?

3. Who made the animals?

4. Are you happy God made all of these?

5. Have you thanked Him?

思考題 Something to Do

當你看到月亮，要感謝天父。
當你看到星星，要感謝天父。
更要感謝天父創造了萬物。

When you see the moon, thank God for it.
When you see the stars, thank God for them.
And thank God for other good things too.

認新詞　　*words to know*

亞當	Adam
夏娃	Eve
丈夫	Husband
妻子	Wife
撒但	Satan

錯事，傷心的事

亞當和夏娃受引誘・創世記 3

亞當是夏娃的丈夫。

夏娃是亞當的妻子。

他們有舒適的家園，美好的食物，

還有很多美好的東西。

他們從來不用憂愁。

只有一件東西是他們不能夠得到的。

天父說：「你們一定不能夠吃那棵樹上的果子。」

Something Bad, Something Sad

Adam and Eve's Temptation · Genesis 3

Adam was Eve's husband.

Eve was Adam's wife.

They had a good home. They had good food.

They had many good things.

And they were never sad.

But there was one thing they could not have.

"You must not eat the food on that tree,"

God said.

一直以來，亞當和夏娃都沒有吃那棵樹上的果子。
有一天，撒但對夏娃說：「妳應該嚐一嚐
這美味的果子。」
夏娃知道天父不許她吃那棵樹上的果子。
可是，果子看來很好吃，
撒但也說它很美味。
這樣，夏娃便吃了，
亞當也吃了。
後來，亞當和夏娃知道他們做了錯事。

For a time, Adam and Eve did not eat from it.
Then Satan talked to Eve one day.
"It is good," he said. "You should eat some."
Eve knew that God did not want her to eat
from that tree.
But the food looked good.
And Satan said it was good.
So Eve ate some. Adam ate some, too.
Then Adam and Eve knew that they
had done something bad.

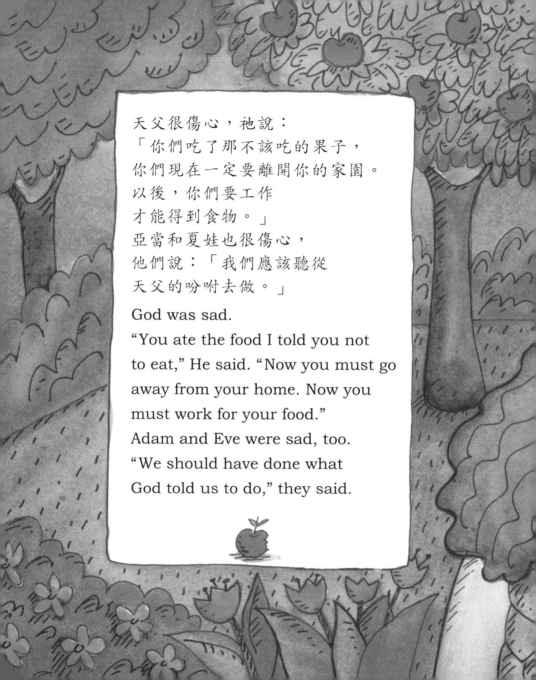

天父很傷心，祂說：
「你們吃了那不該吃的果子，
你們現在一定要離開你的家園。
以後，你們要工作
才能得到食物。」
亞當和夏娃也很傷心，
他們說：「我們應該聽從
天父的吩咐去做。」

God was sad.
"You ate the food I told you not
to eat," He said. "Now you must go
away from your home. Now you
must work for your food."
Adam and Eve were sad, too.
"We should have done what
God told us to do," they said.

問答題 Something to Ask

1. 你有沒有做了一些不應該做的事?

2. 你所做的事討天父的喜悅嗎?

3. 亞當和夏娃有沒有討天父的喜悅?

4. 你為甚麼要做天父喜悅的事?

1. Have you done some things that you should not do?

2. Did these things please God?

3. Did Adam and Eve please God?

4. Why should you try to please God in all you do?

思考題 Something to Do

你怎樣才知道哪些是不對的事？

How do you know when something is bad?

當事情叫別人不開心。

When it makes
others sad.

當天父說這是不對的。

When God says
it is bad.

當爸媽說這是不對的。

When mother and
father say it is bad.

當你知道不應該這樣做。

When you know that
you should not do it.

挪亞造大船

洪水和方舟 · 創世記 6-7

天父說：「造一條大船。」

挪亞說：「是的，我會去造。」

挪亞愛天父，他服從天父，

他會照著天父的話去做。

天父告訴挪亞怎樣去造那條大船。

挪亞用了很長的時間，

按著天父的話把大船造好了。

Noah Makes a Big Boat

The Flood and the Ark · Genesis 6-7

"Make a big boat," God said.

"Yes," said Noah. "I will."

Noah loved God. Noah obeyed God.

He wanted to do what God said.

God told Noah how to make the boat.

Noah made it like God said.

It took a long time.

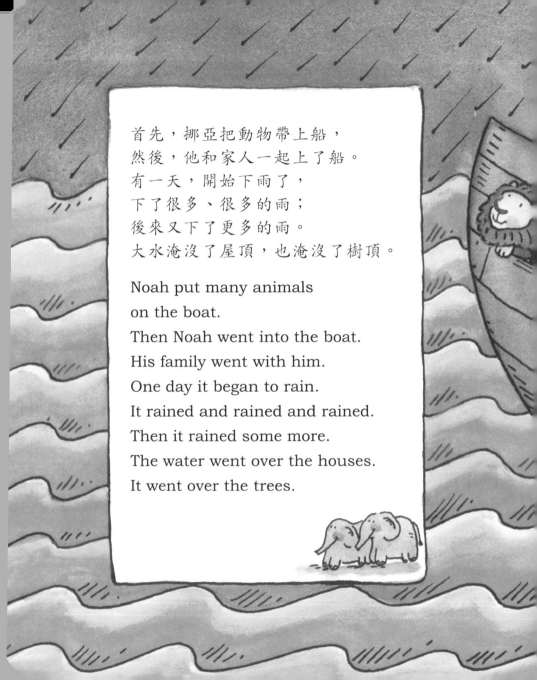

首先，挪亞把動物帶上船，
然後，他和家人一起上了船。
有一天，開始下雨了，
下了很多、很多的雨；
後來又下了更多的雨。
大水淹沒了屋頂，也淹沒了樹頂。

Noah put many animals
on the boat.
Then Noah went into the boat.
His family went with him.
One day it began to rain.
It rained and rained and rained.
Then it rained some more.
The water went over the houses.
It went over the trees.

洪水越漲越高、越漲越高，
很快的，所有的人都不見了。
只有挪亞和他的家人在船上。
挪亞服從天父，所以天父照顧挪亞。
有一天，挪亞說：「感謝天父！」
挪亞感謝天父照顧他。
他感謝天父照顧他的家人。
他感謝天父照顧所有的動物。

The water went higher and higher and higher.

Soon there were no more people.

But Noah and his family were in the boat.

Noah had obeyed God.

So God took care of Noah.

"Thank you, God," Noah said one day.

Noah thanked God for taking care of him.

He thanked God for taking care of his family.

He thanked God for taking care of the animals.

問答題 Something to Ask

1. 是誰照顧你呢?

2. 你有沒有感謝你的爸爸、媽媽?

3. 你有沒有感謝天父?

4. 你有沒有感謝其他人?

1. Who takes care of you?

2. Have you thanked your mother and father?

3. Have you thanked God?

4. Have you thanked others?

思考題 Something to Do

這裡有幾個方法說感謝：

Here are some ways to say thanks:

對別人說：「謝謝你。」
Say thank you to others.

熱心幫助別人。
Do something good
for others.

告訴別人你愛他們。
Tell others that
you love them.

謝恩的日子

挪亞敬拜天父 · 創世記 8

整個世界都給洪水淹沒了。

但是，挪亞和他的家人卻沒有受傷害。

天父告訴挪亞造一條大船。

祂要挪亞把他的家人，和那些

大大、小小的動物一起帶上船。

天父看顧著他們。

A Time to Say Thank You

Noah Worships God · Genesis 8

There was water over all the world.

But Noah and his family did not get hurt.

God had told Noah to make a big boat.

He told Noah to take his family on the big boat.

He told Noah to take many animals, too.

God was taking care of them all.

他們在船上住了一段很長的日子。
有一天，挪亞往船外張望，
看見洪水已經退了。
是天父把洪水帶走的。
挪亞說：「我們一定要感謝天父的幫助。」
挪亞和他的家人一起向天父說感謝。

They were in the boat for many days.
One day Noah looked out of the big boat.
The water was all gone.
God had taken it away.
"We must thank God for helping us," said Noah.
Noah and his family said thank you to God.

天父很高興。

祂在天空中畫了一道彩虹。

天父說：「這道彩虹
是我給你們的應許，我以後再
不會讓洪水淹沒這個世界。」
挪亞很高興聽到天父的應許。
他很高興自己向天父謝了恩。

God was pleased. He made a
rainbow for them to see.
"The rainbow will tell you about
My promise," God said. "I will not
send water over all the world
anymore." Noah was happy to
hear God's promise. He was
happy that he had said thank you
to God!

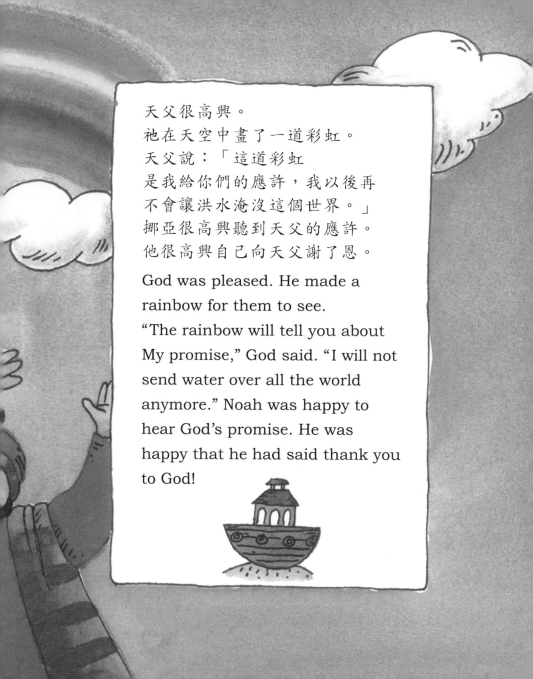

問答題 Something to Ask

1. 挪亞怎樣感謝天父？

2. 他為甚麼要這樣做？

3. 天父後來做了甚麼？

4. 天父賜給你那麼多美好的東西，
   你會怎樣感謝祂？

1. How did Noah thank God?

2. Why did he do this?

3. What did God do then?

4. How can you thank God for the good
   things He has done for you?

思考題 Something to Do

你有沒有感謝天父賜給你……

Do you thank God for...

天父的家? God's house?

你的家? Your house?

你的食物? Your food?

你的爸媽? Mother and father?

你所有的東西?

你的朋友們?

你家中其他的人?

Your things?

Your friends?

Others in your family?

給亞伯拉罕的應許

亞伯拉罕和撒拉的兒子·創世記 18, 21

亞伯拉罕和撒拉都愛天父。

他們向天父禱告。

他們要討天父的喜悅。

天父也愛亞伯拉罕和撒拉。

祂賜給他們很多美好的東西。

但有一些東西是亞伯拉罕和撒拉沒有的；

他們沒有兒子。

認新詞	*words to know*
亞伯拉罕	Abraham
撒拉	Sarah
禱告	Pray
以撒	Isaac
數算	Count

A Promise for Abraham

A Son for Abraham and Sarah · Genesis 18, 21

Abraham and Sarah loved God.

They prayed to God.

They wanted to please God.

God loved Abraham and Sarah, too.

He gave them many good things.

But there was one thing Abraham and Sarah
did not have. They did not have a son.

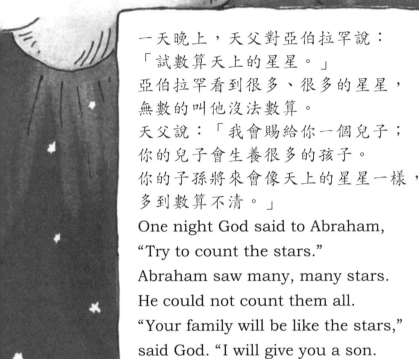

一天晚上，天父對亞伯拉罕說：
「試數算天上的星星。」
亞伯拉罕看到很多、很多的星星，
無數的叫他沒法數算。
天父說：「我會賜給你一個兒子；
你的兒子會生養很多的孩子。
你的子孫將來會像天上的星星一樣，
多到數算不清。」

One night God said to Abraham,
"Try to count the stars."
Abraham saw many, many stars.
He could not count them all.
"Your family will be like the stars,"
said God. "I will give you a son.
Your son will have children.
And some day your family
will be too big to count."

過了一些日子，撒拉有了一個兒子。
亞伯拉罕說：「天父賜給我們這個兒子，
天父照祂的應許做了。」
亞伯拉罕和撒拉替兒子取名叫以撒。
有了這個兒子後，他們非常快樂！
天父也非常快樂。

After a long time, Sarah had a baby boy.
"God did what He promised to do," said Abraham.
"God gave us this baby boy."
Abraham and Sarah gave their boy a name.
"We will call him Isaac," they said.
How happy they were with their baby boy!
And God was happy, too.

問答題 Something to Ask

1. 亞伯拉罕和撒拉怎樣去表示他們愛天父?

2. 你怎樣去表示你愛天父?

3. 天父應許了亞伯拉罕和撒拉些甚麼?

4. 天父有沒有做了祂所應許的事?

5. 天父應許了你甚麼?

6. 你相信天父會照祂的應許去做嗎?

1. How did Abraham and Sarah show that they loved God?

2. How can you show that you love God?

3. What did God promise Abraham and Sarah?

4. Did God do what He promised?

5. What are some of God's promises to you?

6. Do you think that God will do what He promised?

思考題 Something to Do

甚麼是適當的時候去思想天父的應許呢？

When is a good time to think about God's promises?

在晚上。
At night.

當你玩耍時。
When you play.

當你憂傷時。
When you are sad.

當你開心時。
When you are happy.

認新詞　　words to know

雅各　Jacob
天使　Angel
夢　　Dream
梯子　Ladder
天堂　Heaven

雅各看見一道梯子

雅各的夢 · 創世記 27-28

雅各非常憂傷。
他要離開自己的家園，
前往一個很遠的地方。
雅各走了一天的路，
離家已經很遠了。
他一直走到晚上才停下來。

Jacob Sees a Ladder

Jacob's Dream · Genesis 27-28

Jacob was very sad.

He had to go away from home.

He had to go far away.

So Jacob walked all day.

He walked far from home.

When it was night he stopped.

一天晚上，雅各做了一個夢，
他看見一道梯子，一直達到天堂。
許多天使在梯子上，上下往來。
跟著，天父對雅各說話。
祂說：「我會和你一起走，
我會幫助你。」

One night Jacob had a dream.
He saw a ladder.
It went all the way to heaven.
Angels went up and down
on the ladder.
Then God talked to Jacob.
"I will go with you," God said.
"I will help you."

雅各夢醒以後，坐了起來。
他說：「天父剛才在這裡，
祂會和我一起走。」
雅各很快樂。
他很想天父和他一起走。
他很想天父幫助他。

Jacob stopped dreaming.
He sat up.
"God was here," he said.
"And God will go with me."
Jacob was happy.
He wanted God to go with him.
He wanted God to help him.

問答題 Something to Ask

1. 雅各看見些甚麼？

2. 梯子一直達到哪裡去？

3. 誰在梯子上行走？

4. 誰跟雅各說話？

5. 天父說了些甚麼？

6. 雅各為甚麼覺得快樂？

1. What did Jacob see?

2. Where did the ladder go?

3. Who was on the ladder?

4. Who talked to Jacob?

5. What did God say?

6. Why was Jacob happy?

思考題 Something to Do

天父有沒有和你在一起？
你希望天父和你在一起嗎？
你想現在就求告祂嗎？

Is God with you?
Would you like Him to be with you?
Will you ask Him now?

天父看顧約瑟

約瑟在埃及 · 創世記 37-41

約瑟的兄弟們不喜歡他，
他們想傷害他。
其中一個哥哥說：「讓我們
把約瑟殺掉吧！」
另外一個哥哥說：「不，讓我們把他賣了做奴僕；
他會不停地工作、工作、工作！」
約瑟的兄弟們真的把他賣了，
但是，天父看顧約瑟。

God Takes Care of Joseph

Joseph in Egypt · Genesis 37-41

Joseph's brothers did not like him.

They wanted to hurt him.

"Let's kill Joseph," said one brother.

"No," said another brother.

"Let's sell him. He will be a slave.

He will have to work and work and work."

Joseph's brothers DID sell him.

But God took care of Joseph.

51

後來，壞事發生了；
有人把約瑟關在監牢裡，
但是，天父看顧約瑟。
一天晚上，國王做了一個夢。
國王問：「這個夢是甚麼意思？」
可是，沒有人能告訴他。
一個曾經和約瑟一起坐牢的人說：
「約瑟可以告訴你。」
這樣，國王便召見了約瑟。

Then something bad happened.

A man put Joseph in jail.

But God took care of Joseph.

One night the king had a dream.

"What does the dream mean?" the king asked.

No one could tell him.

"Joseph can tell you," said a man.

He had been in jail with Joseph.

The king sent for Joseph.

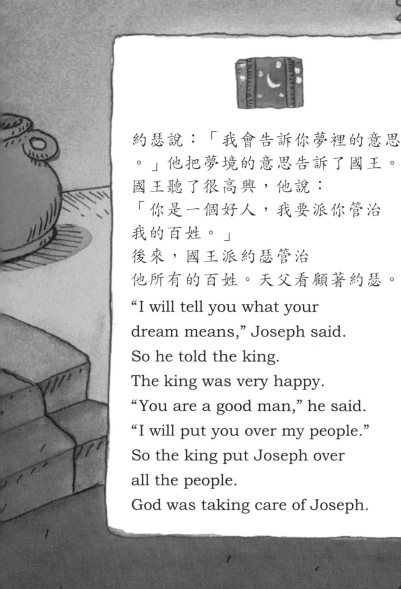

約瑟說：「我會告訴你夢裡的意思。」他把夢境的意思告訴了國王。國王聽了很高興，他說：「你是一個好人，我要派你管治我的百姓。」
後來，國王派約瑟管治他所有的百姓。天父看顧著約瑟。

"I will tell you what your
dream means," Joseph said.
So he told the king.
The king was very happy.
"You are a good man," he said.
"I will put you over my people."
So the king put Joseph over
all the people.
God was taking care of Joseph.

問答題 Something to Ask

1. 約瑟的兄弟們怎樣傷害他？

2. 天父怎樣看顧約瑟？

3. 天父怎樣看顧你？

4. 你有沒有求天父這樣做？

1. How did Joseph's brothers hurt him?

2. How did God take care of Joseph?

3. How does God take care of you?

4. Do you ask God to do this?

思考題 Something to Do

在紙上寫下「請求」兩個字。

把它放在你每天都可以看見的地方。

當你看見「請求」兩個字時，馬上求天父幫助你。

Write ASK on some paper.

Put it where you can see it each day.

When you see ASK, ask God to help you.

約瑟饒恕了他的兄弟

約瑟和兄弟團聚．創世記 42-45

約瑟的兄弟們對他做了不應該做的事；
他們把約瑟賣掉了，
這樣，約瑟變成了奴僕。
但是，天父看顧約瑟。
天父幫助約瑟解開國王的夢；
國王派約瑟管治他所有的百姓。

認新詞 | words to know

饒恕 Forgive
穀物 Grain
賣 Sold
以為 Thought
倒轉 Turn

Joseph Forgives His Brothers

Joseph and His Brothers Reunited · Genesis 42-45

Joseph's brothers had been mean to him.

They sold him, so Joseph became a slave.

But God took care of Joseph.

He helped Joseph tell the king about his dream.

So the king put Joseph over all his people.

有一天，約瑟的兄弟們來找他；
他們不知道他就是約瑟。
約瑟的兄弟們想買些穀物，
約瑟把穀物賣了給他們帶回家。

One day Joseph's brothers
came to see him.
They did not know that he
was Joseph.
Joseph's brothers wanted to
buy grain.
Joseph sold them grain
to take home.

過了一些日子，他們再回來；
他們要多買一些穀物。
這時，約瑟便告訴了兄弟們他是誰。
兄弟們聽了都很害怕，
以為約瑟要把他們殺死，
但是，約瑟並沒有這樣做。
約瑟說：「我饒恕你們。」
這件事討天父的喜悅。
天父要我們饒恕別人，
因為祂也饒恕了我們。

After many days they came back.
They wanted to buy more grain.
Then Joseph told them who he was.
Joseph's brothers were afraid.
They thought Joseph would kill them.
But he did not want to do that.
"I forgive you," said Joseph.
This pleased God.
God wants us to forgive others.
He forgives us, too.

問答題 Something to Ask

1. 約瑟的兄弟們對他做了些甚麼?

2. 他們是不是對約瑟做了不應該做的事?

3. 約瑟有沒有饒恕他的兄弟們?

4. 你認為這件事會討天父的喜悅嗎?

1. What did Joseph's brothers do to him?
2. Were they mean to Joseph?
3. Did Joseph forgive his brothers?
4. Do you think that pleased God?

思考題 Something to Do

下面的題目缺少了哪一個字?

約瑟會_____ 他的兄弟們。

天父會_____ 你。

Which word is not here?

Joseph wanted to _____ his brothers.

God wants to _____ you.

(把圖中的字倒轉過來看。)

(Turn this over to see the word.)

米利暗是勇敢的女孩子

籃子裡的嬰孩摩西 · 出埃及記 2

國王不喜歡米利暗的族人，
他想把他們所有的男嬰殺死。
米利暗的媽媽說：「千萬不要讓國王
的手下找到我們的嬰孩。可是，我們可以
把他藏在哪裡呢？如果把他藏在家裡，
國王的手下一定會找到他的。」
後來，米利暗的媽媽造了一個籃子。
她說：「我們把他放在籃子裡吧！」

Miriam Is a Brave Girl

The Baby Moses in the Basket · Exodus 2

The king did not like Miriam's people.
He wanted to kill all their baby boys.
"The king's men must not find our baby,"
said Miriam's mother.
"But where can we put him? If we put him in our house,
the king's men will find him."
Miriam's mother made a basket.
"We will put him in this," she said.

跟著，她把籃子放在河邊。

米利暗說：「我會和我們的嬰孩在一起。」

米利暗是勇敢的女孩子。

過了一會兒，公主來到河邊洗澡。

公主對她的僕人說：「河邊有一個籃子，
快拿來給我。」

公主看見籃子裡的嬰孩，

她說：「我要收養這個嬰孩，
可是，我要找人來照顧他。」

Then she put the basket on the river.

"I will stay with our baby," said Miriam.

She was a brave girl.

Soon a woman came to the river to wash.

She was the princess.

"A basket!" the princess said to her helpers.

"Go get it for me."

The princess looked in the basket.

She said, "I will keep this baby.

But I want someone to take care of him."

米利暗跑到公主面前說：
「我知道有人可以幫忙，
我的媽媽可以照顧他。」
米利暗的媽媽非常高興，
她知道國王的手下，
再不會傷害她的嬰孩了。
她說：「米利暗，謝謝妳！
我勇敢的好助手。」

Miriam ran to the princess.
"I know someone who
will do it," she said.
"My mother will take care of him."
Miriam's mother was so happy.
The king's men could not hurt
her baby now.
She said, "Thank you, Miriam,
for being my brave helper."

問答題 Something to Ask

1. 國王想做些甚麼?

2. 米利暗做了哪些勇敢的事?

3. 你怎樣才能像米利暗一樣呢?

1. What did the king want to do?

2. What did Miriam do that was brave?

3. How can you be like Miriam?

思考題 Something to Do

你在甚麼時候需要有勇氣?
誰能增加你的勇氣?

When should you be brave?
Who can help you be brave?

天父對摩西說話

摩西和燃燒中的矮樹‧出埃及記 2-4

公主在籃子裡找到一個嬰孩，
她替他取名叫摩西。
摩西現在已經是一個男子漢，
他住在埃及。
可是，國王要殺害他，
所以他要逃命。
摩西要逃到離家很遠的地方去牧羊。

God Talks
to Moses

Moses and the Burning Bush · Exodus 2-4

The princess found a baby in a basket.

She named him Moses.

Moses was now a man.

He lived in Egypt.

But the king wanted to kill him, so he ran away.

Moses took care of his sheep

far away from his home.

摩西看著他的羊兒說：
「我的羊兒很快樂，
可是，我的族人不快樂，
他們被人當作奴僕。」
忽然，摩西看見一棵矮樹在火中燃燒，
但是沒有被燒燬。
天父從矮樹中對摩西說：「回到埃及去，
帶領我的子民離開那地方，
他們不可以再替國王做工了。」

Moses looked at his sheep.

"My sheep are happy," he said.

"But my people are not happy.

They are slaves."

Then Moses saw a bush.

It was burning. But it did not burn up.

God talked to Moses from the bush.

"Go back to Egypt," God said.

"Lead my people away from there.

They must not work for the king anymore."

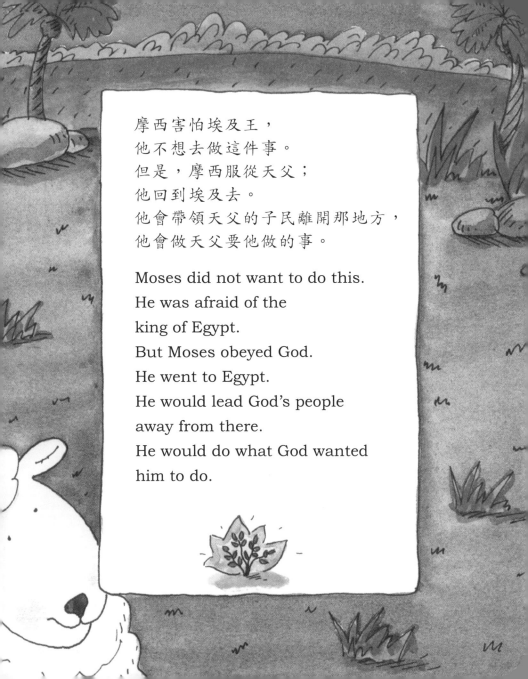

摩西害怕埃及王，
他不想去做這件事。
但是，摩西服從天父；
他回到埃及去。
他會帶領天父的子民離開那地方，
他會做天父要他做的事。

Moses did not want to do this.
He was afraid of the
king of Egypt.
But Moses obeyed God.
He went to Egypt.
He would lead God's people
away from there.
He would do what God wanted
him to do.

問答題 Something to Ask

1. 摩西看見些甚麼？

2. 天父要摩西做些甚麼？

3. 摩西為甚麼害怕？國王想做甚麼？

4. 摩西為甚麼要回到埃及？

5. 他會在那裡做些甚麼？

1. What did Moses see?

2. What did God tell Moses to do?

3. Why was Moses afraid?
   What did the king want to do?

4. Why did Moses go back to Egypt?

5. What would he do there?

思考題 Something to Do

誰是你應該服從的？

Who should you obey?

媽媽? Mother?

爸爸? Father?

天父? God?

壞朋友? Bad friends?

一個說「不」的國王

法老和摩西 · 出埃及記 5-12

摩西說：「讓天父的子民離去，
不要再叫他們替你做工！」
國王說：「不可以！」
摩西說：「天父說你一定要這樣做。」
國王說：「我不會聽從你天父的話。」

認新詞　words to know
休息　Rest
發生　Happen

A King Who Said No

Pharaoh and Moses · Exodus 5-12

"Let God's people go!" said Moses.
"Stop making them do your work."
"No!" said the king.
"God says you must," said Moses.
"But I do not do what your God tells me,"
the king said.

摩西把這話對國王說了很多遍，
可是，國王不聽從天父的話。
國王說：「不可以！」
國王要天父的子民替他做工。
他們得到很少的休息，
他們得到很少的食物。

Time after time Moses talked
to the king.
But the king would not do what
God said.
"No," the king said.
The king made God's people do
all his work.
They did not get much rest.
They did not get much to eat.

後來，天父告訴了摩西怎樣做。
祂說：「回去告訴國王，叫他讓
我的子民離開，否則災難就要發生了。」
可是，國王沒有聽從天父的話。
後來，天父傷害了國王和他的百姓。
國王害怕了。
他對摩西說：「帶領你的族人離開！」
這樣，摩西和他的族人便一起前往新家園。
他們遠離那個對天父說「不」的國王。

Then God told Moses what to do.
"Go back to the king.
Tell him to let My people go
or bad things will happen."
But the king did not obey God.
So God hurt the king and He hurt the king's people.
The king was afraid.
He said, "Take your people and go away!"
So Moses and his people went to a new home.
They went far from the king who said no to God.

問答題 Something to Ask

1. 摩西要求國王做些甚麼?

2. 國王為甚麼說不可以?

3. 甚麼事叫國王說可以?

4. 你怎樣對天父說可以?

1. What did Moses want the king to do?

2. Why did the king say no?

3. What made the king say yes?

4. How can you say yes to God?

思考題 Something to Do

誰在這裡向天父說「不」？

Who is saying no to God here?

我現在不向天父禱告。
I will not talk to
God now.

我要去天父的家。
I want to go to
God's house.

我不聽從媽媽的話。
I will not do what
mother says.

請告訴我耶穌的事。
Please tell me
about Jesus.

認新詞　*words to know*

邊　Side
雲　Cloud
火　Fire
乾　Dry
地方　Place

離開埃及

出埃及記 · 出埃及記 13-15

摩西帶領天父的子民離開埃及，
他們急急的往前走。
百姓都知道天父與他們同行。
每天，天父在雲柱中與他們同行；
每夜，那雲柱像一團火照亮他們。
天父和祂的子民常常在一起，
祂要指引他們的路。

Going Out of Egypt

The Exodus · Exodus 13-15

God's people went away from Egypt.

They went as fast as they could go.

Moses led them.

The people knew that God was with them.

Each day, in a cloud, God was with the people.

Each night the cloud was like fire.

God was with the people all the time.

He was showing them where to go.

91

有一天，百姓來到大海旁邊，
他們不能從水面上走過去，
又不能環繞著海邊走。
國王和他的手下在後面追趕。
他們要殺死天父的子民。
這時，天父把兩旁的海水升高，
在海中開出了一片乾的地方。
摩西帶領著百姓在乾地上走過了大海。

One day the people came to a big sea.

They could not go over it.

They could not go around it.

The king and his men were coming fast.

They wanted to kill God's people.

But God made a dry place to walk in the sea.

On one side the water was high.

On the other side the water was high.

But there was a dry place

where the people could walk.

Moses led the people through the sea.

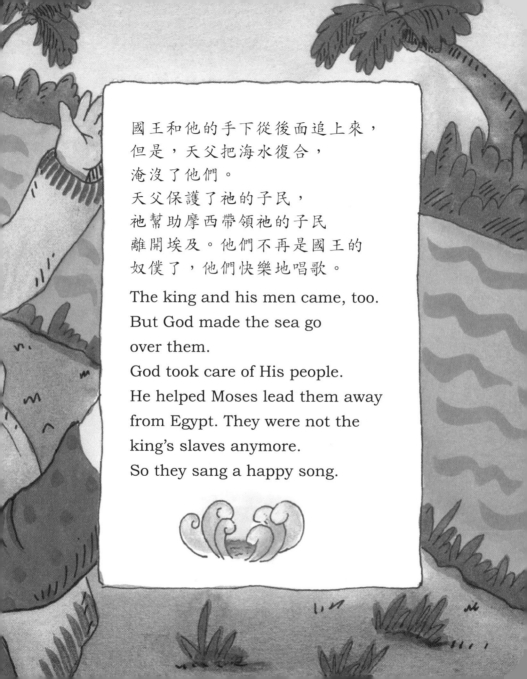

國王和他的手下從後面追上來，
但是，天父把海水復合，
淹沒了他們。
天父保護了祂的子民，
祂幫助摩西帶領祂的子民
離開埃及。他們不再是國王的
奴僕了，他們快樂地唱歌。

The king and his men came, too.
But God made the sea go
over them.
God took care of His people.
He helped Moses lead them away
from Egypt. They were not the
king's slaves anymore.
So they sang a happy song.

問答題 Something to Ask

1. 天父的子民為甚麼要離開埃及？

2. 誰帶領他們？

3. 百姓怎麼知道天父和他們在一起？

4. 他們怎樣走過大海？

5. 天父有沒有看顧他們？你怎麼知道？

1. Why did the people want to go away from Egypt?

2. Who led them?

3. How did the people know that God was with them?

4. How did they get across the sea?

5. Did God take care of them? How do you know?

思考題 Something to Do

天父看顧祂的子民，他們向天父歌唱。
God took care of the people.
So they sang a song for Him.

天父有看顧你嗎? Does God take care of you?

你會向天父歌唱嗎? Will you sing a happy song for Him?

清涼的水，美味的食物

曠野裡的嗎哪和水・出埃及記 15-16

一個小女孩說：「我想喝水。」
她的爸爸說：「我們都想喝水，
可是，這裡沒有水。
我們現在不是在埃及做奴僕了，
可是，我們在這裡不能夠找到水。」
後來，有人急忙的跑來，
他說：「水！我看見有水！」

Something to Drink, Something to Eat

Water and Manna in the Wilderness・Exodus 15-16

"I want some water," a little girl said.

"We want water, too," said her father.

"But there is no water.

We are not slaves in Egypt now.

But we cannot find water."

Then someone ran fast.

"Water!" he said. "I see water!"

所有的人都跑去取水，
可是，那些水是不清潔的、
是不能飲用的。
天父說：「把那棵樹砍下來，
把它放在水裡。」
摩西照天父的話去做，
馬上的，那些水可以飲用了。

All the people went to get
some water.
But they could not drink it.
It was not good water.
"Cut down that tree," God said,
"and put it into the water."
Moses did what God said.
Now the water was good to drink.

一個小男孩說：「我想吃東西。」
他的媽媽說：「我們都想吃東西，
可是，這裡沒有食物。」
摩西說：「天父會賜給你們食物。」
馬上的，天父賜很多小鳥給他們作食物，
每天又賜給他們叫嗎哪的麵包。
他們的食物和我們的食物不同；
但那些好吃的食物，是天父賜給祂的子民的。
天父就是這樣的去照顧祂的子民。

"I want something to eat," a little boy said.

"We want something to eat, too," said his mother.

"But there is no food."

"God will give you food," said Moses.

So God sent birds for the people to eat.

He sent bread each day. It was called manna.

Their food was not like our food.

But it was good food.

God gave it to His people.

That is how God took care of His people.

問答題 Something to Ask

1. 曠野裡為甚麼沒有食物和水?

2. 天父怎樣把不潔淨的水變為潔淨?

3. 天父供應了怎樣的麵包?名稱是甚麼?

4. 天父還供應了哪些食物?

1. Why was there no food or water?

2. How did God make the bad water become good water?

3. What kind of bread did God send? What was it called?

4. What other food did God send?

思考題 Something to Do

請媽媽幫你在家裡找一找：
你可以找到哪幾種食物？
天父的子民有哪幾種食物？
你會感謝天父賜給你美好的食物嗎？

Look in your house. Ask your mother to help you.
How many kinds of food can you find?

How many kinds did God's people have?

Will you thank God for your good food?

天父的誡命

十誡 · 出埃及記 19-20

有些人問：「這是甚麼？」
有些人說：「是打雷！」
其他的人說：「是閃電！」
百姓走近一座高山，他們很害怕。
但是，摩西和他們在一起。
天父幫助摩西帶領祂的子民，
祂幫助摩西把百姓帶到這個地方來。

God's Good Rules

The Ten Commandments · Exodus 19-20

"What is it?" some people asked.

"Thunder!" some said.

"Lightning!" others said.

The people were near a big mountain.

They were afraid.

But Moses was there with them.

God had helped Moses lead the people.

He had helped Moses take them to this place.

天父吩咐摩西到山上去，
摩西服從天父，
他要聽天父的吩咐。
天父對摩西說話；
祂交給摩西一些誠命。
祂說：「告訴我的子民
要遵守這些誠命。」

God told Moses to go up
on the mountain.
Moses obeyed God.
He wanted to hear what God
would say.
God talked with Moses.
He gave Moses some good rules.
He said, "Tell My people to obey
these rules."

天父的誡命： 1. 要敬拜天父。
2. 不可造偶像。
3. 不可亂說天父的名字。
4. 要守安息日。
5. 要服從和愛你的爸爸、媽媽。
6. 不可殺人。
7. 愛你的丈夫或妻子。
8. 不可偷東西。
9. 不可說謊話。
10. 不可貪別人的東西。

These are God's good rules:

1. Worship only God.
2. Do not make something and think it is God.
3. Do not say God's name in a bad way.
4. Rest on God's day.
5. Love and obey your mother and father.
6. Do not kill people.
7. Love your wife or husband.
8. Do not steal.
9. Do not lie.
10. Do not want what others have.

問答題 Something to Ask

1. 天父交給摩西哪些誡命？

2. 你應該遵守這些誡命嗎？

3. 你遵守這些誡命是要討誰的喜悅？

1. What good rules did God give Moses?

2. Should you obey these rules, too?

3. Who will you please if you obey these rules?

思考題 Something to Do

天父把祂的意願告訴摩西和祂的子民。

天父對摩西說話。

天父現在怎樣把祂的意願告訴我們?

祂會在哪裡把祂的意願告訴我們?

God told Moses and His people what He wanted.

He talked to Moses.

How does God tell us now what He wants?

Where does He tell us what He wants?

金牛像

以色列人拜偶像．出埃及記 32

摩西問：「你們會照天父的話去做嗎?」

百姓說：「會，我們會照天父的話去做。」

這樣，摩西便離開了。他要向天父禱告。

摩西離開了一段很長的時間。

有些人說：「摩西不會再回來了，

我們一定要另外找人來幫助。」

A Calf of Gold

Israel Worships an Idol · Exodus 32

"Will you do what God says?" Moses asked.

"Yes," said the people.

"We will do what God says."

Moses went away.

He went to talk with God.

Moses was gone for a long time.

"Moses will not come back," some people said.

"We must have someone to help us."

115

後來，百姓用黃金造了一個金牛像。
他們說：「這個金牛像會幫助我們，
它就是我們的神。」
這些人沒有照天父的話去做，
他們沒有討天父的喜悅。
有一天，摩西回來了，
他不喜歡百姓所做的事，
他說：「你們要討天父的喜悅嗎？
到我這邊來吧！」

So the people made a calf from gold.

"This gold calf will help us," they said.

"It will be our god now."

But the people were not doing what God said.

They were not pleasing God.

One day Moses came back.

He did not like what the people were doing.

"Do you want to please God?" he asked.

"Come here!"

那些想討天父喜悅的人
都跟隨了摩西。
可是，有些人沒有跟隨他。
後來，有些事情發生在那些
壞人身上，他們都死了。
對那些不服從天父的人來說，
那是一個悲傷的日子。

The people who wanted to
please God came to Moses.
But some would not come.
Then something happened to
the bad people.
The bad people died.
It was a sad day for the people
who said no to God.

問答題 Something to Ask

1. 百姓做了甚麼壞事?

2. 天父喜歡他們的金牛像嗎?

3. 你有沒有做了一些天父不高興的事?

4. 你應該怎樣處理這些事呢?

1. What did the people do that was bad?

2. How did God like their gold calf?

3. Is God not happy about some things you do?

4. What should you do about these things?

思考題 Something to Do

你應該在甚麼時候照天父的意願去做?
When should you do what God wants?

有些時候? Some of the time?

時常都做? All of the time?

從來不做? None of the time?

認新詞　words to know

蛇　Snake
銅　Brass
後悔　Sorry
發怒　Angry
懲罰　Punish

天父的子民後悔了

曠野舉銅蛇 · 民數記 21

有些百姓對摩西說：
「你為甚麼把我們帶到這裡來？
我們不喜歡這些食物。」
其他的人說：「天父沒有幫助我們。」
摩西聽了這些話很憂傷。
天父的子民已經不在埃及做奴僕了。
天父幫助摩西帶領祂的子民到這裡來，
賜給他們美好的食物。

God's People Are Sorry

The Bronze Serpent · Numbers 21

"Why did you lead us here?"
some people said to Moses.
"We do not like our food."
Others said, "God does not help us."
Moses was sad to hear these things.
God's people were not slaves in Egypt now.
God had helped Moses lead His people here.
He had given them good food.

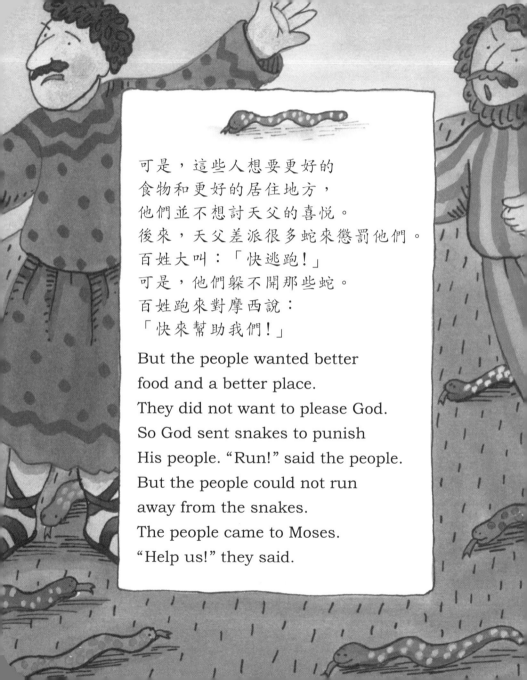

可是，這些人想要更好的
食物和更好的居住地方，
他們並不想討天父的喜悅。
後來，天父差派很多蛇來懲罰他們。
百姓大叫：「快逃跑！」
可是，他們躲不開那些蛇。
百姓跑來對摩西說：
「快來幫助我們！」

But the people wanted better
food and a better place.
They did not want to please God.
So God sent snakes to punish
His people. "Run!" said the people.
But the people could not run
away from the snakes.
The people came to Moses.
"Help us!" they said.

摩西為了這件事向天父禱告。
天父對摩西說：「造一條大銅蛇，
把它掛在高處，讓大家都看見，
誰看見它就不會死。」
摩西照著天父的話去做，
那些看見銅蛇的人真的沒有死去。
這就是一個用來表示百姓後悔的方法，
天父會幫助他們，祂會饒恕他們。

Moses talked to God about this.

"Make a big brass snake," God told Moses.

"Put it up high for the people to see.

People who look at it will not die."

Moses did what God told him to do.

The people who looked at the snake did not die.

That was a way to say they were sorry.

Then God would help them.

He would forgive them.

問答題 Something to Ask

1. 百姓想要甚麼？

2. 天父為甚麼對這件事情發怒？

3. 天父怎樣懲罰他們？

4. 這些人怎樣去表示後悔？

1. What did the people want?

2. Why was God angry about that?

3. How did God punish them?

4. How could the people say they were sorry?

思考題 Something to Do

用紙寫上「錯事」，「後悔」和「禱告」幾個字。
把紙放在你每天都可以看見的地方。
當你做了錯事的時候，看看這些字。
你有後悔嗎？趕快禱告吧！

Put BAD, SORRY, and PRAY on some paper.
Put this where you will see it each day.
When you do something bad, look at it.
Are you sorry? Then pray.

認新詞　words to know

耶利哥　Jericho
約書亞　Joshua
城牆　Walls
七　Seven
攻打　Fight

天父幫助約書亞
耶利哥的城牆 · 約書亞記 6

天父的子民說：「看那些城牆，
我們怎能攻打耶利哥城的人？
我們怎能夠爬過那些城牆？」
約書亞說：「天父會幫助我們。」
天父真的幫助了約書亞。
祂告訴約書亞怎樣去攻打耶利哥城。
約書亞告訴了百姓，
他們就照著這個辦法去做。

God Helps Joshua
The Walls of Jericho · Joshua 6

"Look at those walls," said God's people.

"How can we fight the people of Jericho?

How can we get over those walls?"

"God will help us," said Joshua.

God DID help Joshua.

He told Joshua how to fight Jericho.

Then Joshua told the people.

This is the way they did it.

約書亞和百姓圍繞耶利哥城
走了一圈，就回家去了。
第二天，他們照樣繞城走一圈。
他們每天都做同樣的事。
耶利哥城裡的人都說：
「他們在做甚麼？
他們為甚麼不攻打我們？」
Joshua and the people went
around the walls of Jericho.
Then they went home.
The next day they went
around the walls again.
They did this each day.
"What are they doing?"
asked the people of Jericho.
"Why don't they fight us?"

有一天，約書亞和百姓
圍繞城牆走了一圈又一圈，
一直繞了七次，就停了下來。
耶利哥城裡的人都害怕了。
跟著發生了甚麼事情呢？
約書亞和百姓向城牆高聲喊叫，
耶利哥的城牆就倒了下來。
約書亞和百姓跑進城裡，把它佔領了。
約書亞說：「是天父幫助我們做這件事。」

One day Joshua and the people
went around and around the walls.
They went around the walls seven times.
Then they stopped.
The people of Jericho were afraid.
What would happen now?
Joshua and the people began to shout.
The walls of Jericho fell down.
Joshua and the people ran into Jericho
and took it.
"God helped us do this," Joshua said.

問答題 Something to Ask

1. 誰告訴約書亞怎樣攻下耶利哥城？

2. 約書亞有沒有服從天父？

3. 約書亞怎樣攻下耶利哥城？

1. Who told Joshua how to take Jericho?
2. Did Joshua obey God?
3. How did Joshua take Jericho?

思考題 Something to Do

你希望天父幫助你做些甚麼？

你想現在就求祂幫助你嗎？

What would you like God to help you do?

Will you ask Him to help you now?

蒙天父賜強壯的人

參孫‧士師記 13-16

參孫是最強壯的人。這是天父的恩賜。

參孫力氣很大，

他用雙手就能殺死獅子。

有些人想殺害參孫；

他們不喜歡參孫的族人。

但是，參孫的力氣實在比他們強大。

A Man Made Strong by God

Samson · Judges 13-16

Samson was the strongest man of all.

God had made him that way.

Samson was so strong that he killed a lion.

He did it with his hands.

Some people tried to kill Samson.

They did not like Samson's people.

But Samson was too strong for them.

後來，參孫做了一些壞事，
是天父不喜悅的。
他所做的事連他的爸爸和媽媽都不喜悅。
參孫做了傷害他自己的事。
天父說：「參孫現在不再強壯了。」
有些人把參孫帶走，
參孫再也不能阻止他們了。

Then Samson did some bad things.
He did things that did not please God.
He did things that did not please
his father and mother.
Samson did things that hurt him.
So God said, "Now Samson will not be strong."
Some people took Samson away.
Samson could not stop them.

141

這些人要參孫替他們做工,
還把他的眼睛弄瞎了。
參孫很悲傷,因為他沒有討天父
的喜悅。
天父賜給參孫很多的恩典,
你認為參孫應該替
天父做些甚麼?

The people made Samson work
for them. They hurt him so that
he could not see.
Then Samson was sad that he
had not pleased God.
God had given Samson so much.
What do you think Samson
should have done for God?

問答題 Something to Ask

1. 天父有沒有賜給你很多好的東西？

2. 你要替祂做些甚麼？

3. 參孫做了些甚麼？

4. 你應該做哪些參孫沒有做過的事？

1. Has God given you many good things?

2. What do you do for Him?

3. What did Samson do?

4. What should you do that Samson
   did not do?

思考題 Something to Do

誰人應該照天父的意願去做？

Who should do what God wants?

一個新家庭
路得跟隨拿俄米・路得記 1-4

拿俄米受盡痛苦。
她的丈夫和兩個兒子都死了。
她想回到自己的家鄉去。
拿俄米說：「我要回家，
回到我的族人那裡去。」
路得說：「我和妳一起回去。」
這樣，路得便跟隨拿俄米回到她的族人那裡去。

認新詞 / *words to know*

拿俄米	Naomi
路得	Ruth
波阿斯	Boaz

A New Family
Ruth Follows Naomi · Ruth 1-4

"I am going home," Naomi said.

"I am going back to my people."

Many things had hurt Naomi.

Her husband had died.

Her sons had died.

Now she wanted to go back to her home.

"I will go with you," said Ruth.

So Ruth went back with Naomi to her people.

147

拿俄米和路得回到家鄉後，
沒有人替她們去找食物，
這樣，路得要出外去尋找。
有一天，路得遇見一個好人，
他的名字叫波阿斯。
波阿斯喜歡路得，
路得也喜歡波阿斯。
波阿斯向路得說：「我可以做妳的丈夫嗎？」

In their new home there was no one
to get food for Ruth and Naomi.
So Ruth went to look for food.
One day Ruth saw a good man.
His name was Boaz.
Boaz loved Ruth.
Ruth loved Boaz.
"May I be your husband?" Boaz asked Ruth.

路得非常高興，
她很高興找到波阿斯做她的丈夫。
她說：「波阿斯愛我，
他會照顧拿俄米和我。」
過了一段日子，
路得和波阿斯有了一個兒子，
他們全家都很快樂。

Ruth was very happy.
She was happy to have Boaz
for her husband.
"Boaz will take care of Naomi
and me," she said.
"And he will love me, too."
After a time, Ruth and Boaz
had a baby boy.
They were a very happy family.

問答題 Something to Ask

1. 路得為甚麼高興？

2. 怎樣才可以成為一個快樂的家庭？

3. 你有一個快樂的家庭嗎？

4. 你能替你的家庭做些甚麼？

5. 這樣做你會感到快樂嗎？

1. Why was Ruth happy?

2. What can make a family happy?

3. Do you have a happy family?

4. What can you do to help your family?

5. Will this make you happy, too?

思考題 Something to Do

家庭是甚麼?

What is a family?

有了這些東西就是一個家庭嗎?

Do these things make a family?

一個家庭真正需要甚麼?

What things DO make a family?

小男孩有一個新的家

撒母耳獻身天父 · 撒母耳記上 1-2

哈拿很想有一個兒子。

她求天父賜給她一個兒子。

哈拿說：「如果祢賜給我一個兒子，

我會要他事奉祢。」

天父答應了哈拿的請求。

哈拿有了兒子後，她非常高興，

她說：「我要替他取名撒母耳，

還要把他獻給天父。」

A Boy Gets a New Home

Samuel Dedicated to God · 1 Samuel 1-2

Hannah wanted a baby so much.

So Hannah asked God for a baby boy.

"If You give me a little boy," said Hannah,

"I will let him do Your work."

God did what Hannah asked.

Hannah was so happy with her baby boy.

"I will call him Samuel," she said.

"And I will give him to God."

155

撒母耳日漸長大，
哈拿帶他到天父的家去見以利。
以利看顧著天父的家。
她向以利說：「你可以幫助我的兒子
去事奉天父嗎？」
以利回答說：「可以。」
這樣，以利便幫助撒母耳去認識天父；
撒母耳也幫助以利看顧天父的家。

When Samuel was bigger,

Hannah took him to God's house.

She talked to Eli, the man who took care of

God's house.

"Will you help my boy do God's work?"

Hannah asked.

"Yes," said Eli.

So Eli helped Samuel to know about God.

And Samuel helped Eli take care of God's house.

157

撒母耳和以利一起住在天父的家，
哈拿來探望他的時候，
都帶給他很多美好的東西。
撒母耳愛他的媽媽，他也愛以利；
他喜歡這個能夠讓他
事奉天父的家。
但最重要的，他愛天父。

Samuel stayed with Eli
at God's house.
Hannah came to see him.
She took him many good things.
Samuel loved his mother.
He loved Eli, too.
And Samuel loved his new home
where he worked for God.
But best of all, he loved God.

問答題 Something to Ask

1. 撒母耳住在哪裡?

2. 他為甚麼住在那地方?

3. 撒母耳為甚麼喜歡他那新的家?

4. 你怎樣才能夠幫助天父去做祂的工作?

1. Where did Samuel live?

2. Why did he live there?

3. Why did Samuel love his new home?

4. How can you help God do His work?

思考題 Something to Do

甚麼時候你可以向天父禱告？

When can you talk to God?

大衛是勇敢的男孩子

大衛與巨人 · 撒母耳記上 17

巨人歌利亞大聲呼叫：
「快出來和我作戰！」
可是，天父的子民都怕歌利亞，
沒有人敢和他作戰。
有一個叫大衛的男孩子說：
「我不怕歌利亞，我要和他作戰。」
國王說：「怎麼可以呢？他比你長得強壯。」
大衛回答說：「天父會幫助我。」

David Is a Brave Boy

David and Goliath · 1 Samuel 17

"Come and fight me," Goliath called.

But not one of God's people would fight him.

They were afraid of Goliath.

A boy named David said,

"I am not afraid. I will fight Goliath."

"How can you?" asked the king.

"You are not as big as he is."

"God will help me," said David.

大衛跑過去迎戰歌利亞，
他拿著他的機弦和五塊石子。
巨人衝向大衛，
想把大衛殺死。
歌利亞的族人也想把
天父的子民殺死。
大衛向天父禱告，
他說：「天父，求祢幫助我。」

So David went to fight Goliath.

He took his sling.

And he took five stones.

The big man ran at David.

He wanted to kill David.

The people with Goliath wanted

to kill God's people, too.

David talked to God.

"Help me, God," he asked.

165

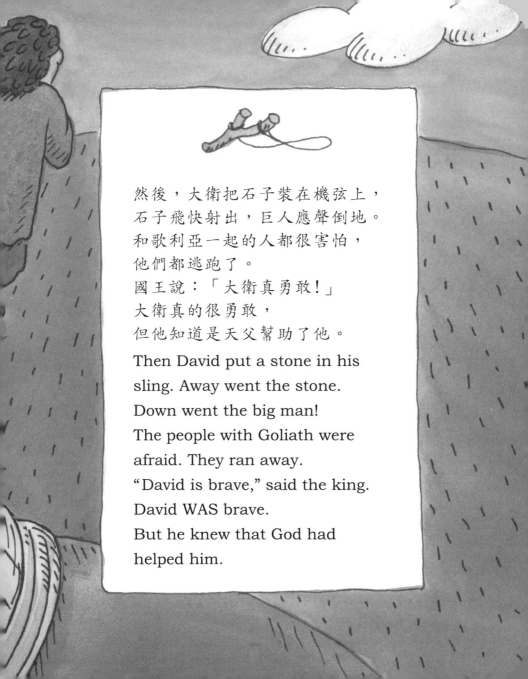

然後，大衛把石子裝在機弦上，
石子飛快射出，巨人應聲倒地。
和歌利亞一起的人都很害怕，
他們都逃跑了。
國王說：「大衛真勇敢！」
大衛真的很勇敢，
但他知道是天父幫助了他。

Then David put a stone in his
sling. Away went the stone.
Down went the big man!
The people with Goliath were
afraid. They ran away.
"David is brave," said the king.
David WAS brave.
But he knew that God had
helped him.

問答題 Something to Ask

1. 巨人歌利亞想做甚麼？

2. 大衛怎樣表現出他的勇氣？

3. 當你需要幫助的時候，
   你會向天父說些甚麼？

1. What did Goliath want to do?

2. How did David show that he was brave?

3. What do you say to God when you
   need help?

思考題 Something to Do

當你覺得不夠勇氣的時候，你應該怎

What should you do when you don't feel brave?

好朋友

大衛和約拿單 · 撒母耳記上 18

認新詞

	words to know
約拿單	Jonathan
寶劍	Sword
弓	Bow
箭	Arrows
外袍	Robe

國王看見大衛殺了歌利亞。

他知道大衛是一個勇敢的男孩子。

國王的兒子也看見這件事，

他的名字叫約拿單，

他也是一個勇敢的男孩子。

約拿單很想跟大衛做朋友。

約拿單問：「你要跟我做好朋友嗎？」

大衛說：「好的，我會跟你做好朋友。」

Good Friends

David and Jonathan · 1 Samuel 18

The king saw David killed Goliath.

He saw that David was a brave boy.

The king's son saw this, too.

His name was Jonathan.

He was a brave boy, too.

Jonathan wanted David to be his friend.

"Will you be my best friend?" Jonathan asked.

"Yes, I will be your best friend," said David.

約拿單有很多好的東西。
他把最好的東西送給大衛：
他把自己的寶劍、弓和箭，
都送了給大衛。

Jonathan had many
good things.
He gave his best things
to David.
He gave David his sword.
He gave David his bow
and arrows.

174

他把自己的外袍送給大衛。
約拿單說：「這是向你表明
我是你的朋友。」
大衛說：「謝謝你美好的禮物，
謝謝你跟我做好朋友！」

He gave David his robe.
"This will show you that I am your friend,"
said Jonathan.
"Thank you for your best things," said David.
"And thank you for being my best friend."

問答題 Something to Ask

1. 約拿單是誰？他的爸爸是誰？

2. 約拿單為甚麼想跟大衛做朋友？

3. 約拿單送了些甚麼東西給大衛？

4. 他為甚麼要這樣做？

1. Who was Jonathan?
   Who was his father?

2. Why did Jonathan want to be David's friend?

3. What did Jonathan give David?

4. Why did he do this?

思考題 Something to Do

好朋友應該做些甚麼？ What should good friends do?

互相打架?
Fight each other?

互相幫助?
Help each other?

給對方送禮物?
Give each other
good things?

給對方說美好的話?
Say good things to
each other?

認新詞 | words to know
所羅門王 | Solomon
智慧 | Wise
婦人 | Women
兩/二 | Two

一位有智慧的國王

判斷精明的所羅門王 · 列王紀上 3

百姓說：「所羅門王萬歲！」
所羅門是新登基的國王，
他是一位非常有智慧的國王。
他曾經求天父賜給他智慧。

A Wise King

Solomon Judges Wisely · 1 Kings 3

"Long live King Solomon!" the people said.

Solomon was the new king.

He was a very wise king.

He had asked God to make him wise.

一天，兩個婦人帶著一個嬰孩
走進來，她們各自說：
「這是我的嬰孩！」
所羅門王不知道
誰是嬰孩的媽媽。
他說：「把嬰孩分成兩半，
各人拿一半吧！」

One day two women came
with a baby. Each woman said,
"This is MY baby!"
Solomon did not know who
was the mother.
"Cut the baby in two," he said.
"Give some of it to each one."

182

嬰孩的媽媽說：「不好！」

另一個婦人說：「好！」

這樣，所羅門王便知道誰是嬰孩真正的媽媽。

他說：「把嬰孩歸給那個婦人。」

百姓說：「我們的國王充滿智慧。」

所羅門王說：「感謝天父給我的指引！」

"No!" said the mother.

"Yes!" said the other woman.

Then Solomon knew who the mother was.

"Give the baby to that woman," he said.

"How wise our king is," said the people.

"Thank you, God, for showing me what to do,"
said King Solomon.

問答題 Something to Ask

1. 所羅門王為甚麼知道怎樣去做？

2. 他怎樣表現出他的智慧？

3. 你想有人幫助你知道怎樣去做嗎？

4. 誰可以幫助你？

5. 你會請求祂嗎？

1. How did Solomon know what to do?

2. How did he show that he was wise?

3. Do you want someone to help you know what to do?

4. Who can help you?

5. Will you ask Him?

思考題 Something to Do

天父要你怎樣去做呢？

What would God want you to do?

這樣…… This...

還是那樣？ or that?

這樣…… This...

還是那樣？ or that?

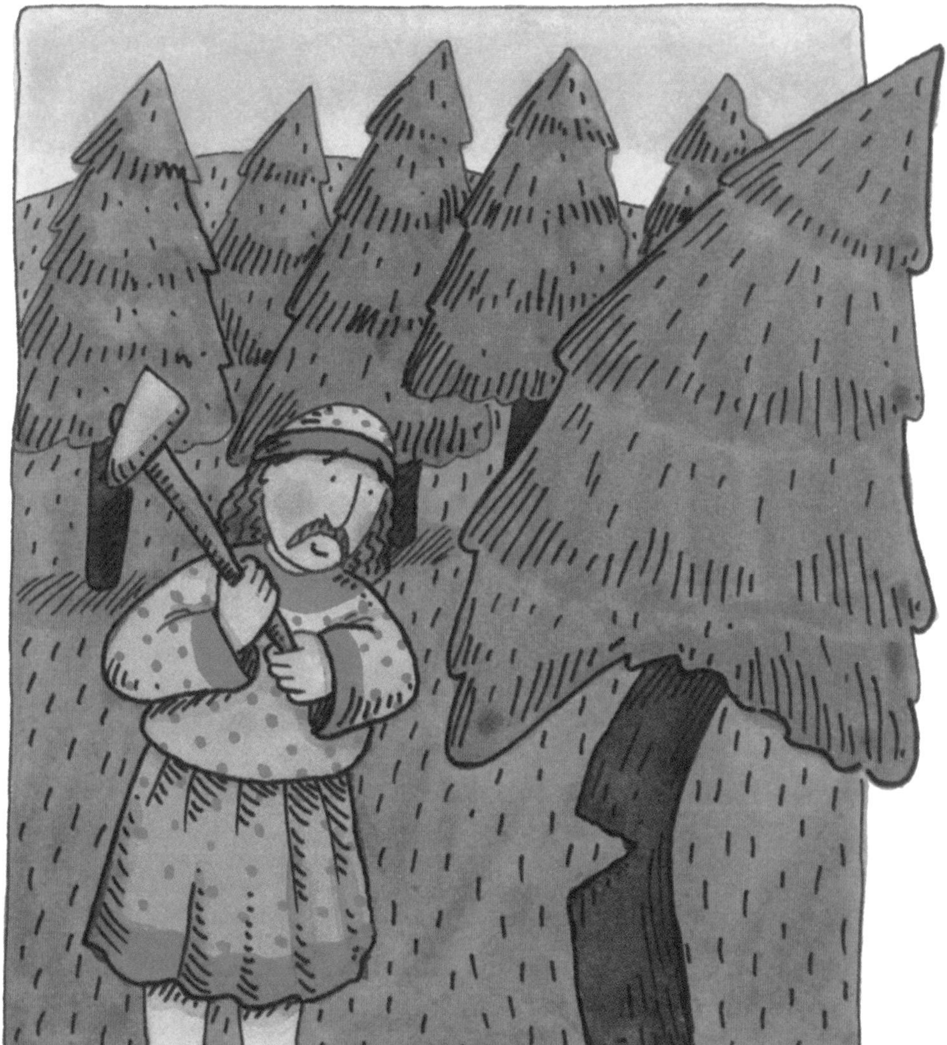

替天父建造華麗的家

所羅門王建造聖殿 · 列王紀上 5-8

有些人問：「所羅門王在做些甚麼？」
另一些人說：「他給天父建造一所
非常華麗的家。」
國王說：「尋找最好的木材來建造天父的家。
天父的家一定要用最好的木材來建造。」
人們跑到遠方去，
他們砍下最好的樹木。

A Beautiful House for God

Solomon Builds the Temple · 1 Kings 5-8

"What is King Solomon doing?" someone asked.

"He is building a house for God," said another.

"It will be very beautiful."

"Find the best trees for God's house," said the king.

"God's house must have the best trees of all."

So men went far away.

They cut the best trees.

其他的人把大石塊鑿開做城牆。
有些東西用黃金來造。
有些東西用布料來造。

Other men cut big stones for the walls.
Some worked with gold.
And some worked with cloth.

189

當人們在天父的家工作時，
他們都很安靜。他們工作了一段
很長的日子，終於把工作完成了。
所羅門王對所有的人說：
「天父的家非常華麗！大家快來看！」
很多人都跑來看，
他們高聲歌唱：「天父真美好！」

When people worked at God's
house, they were very quiet.
People worked for many days.
At last the work was done.
"Come see God's house,"
King Solomon told everyone.
"It is very beautiful!"
Many people came to see it.
"God is good!" they sang.

問答題 Something to Ask

1. 所羅門王建造了甚麼？

2. 所羅門王用好的還是
   用壞的東西來建造？

3. 天父的家落成後，人們做了些甚麼？

1. What did King Solomon build?

2. Did Solomon build it with good things
   or bad things?

3. What did people do when God's
   house was done?

思考題 Something to Do

你在天父的家應該做些甚麼?

哪些是你不應該做的?

What should you do in God's house?

What should you NOT do?

小鳥送食物

天父餵養以利亞·列王紀上　17

以利亞要逃命，
因為他把天父的話告訴了國王。
國王不喜歡聽見天父說他不對的話，
國王想殺死以利亞。
天父說：「你一定要躲避國王。」
以利亞問：「躲到哪裡去？」
天父說：「我會指引你。」

Birds with Food for a Man

God Feeds Elijah · 1 Kings 17

Elijah had to run away.

He had told the king what God said.

But the king did not like what God said.

He did not like to hear how bad he was.

So the king wanted to kill Elijah.

"You must hide from the king," God said.

"Where?" asked Elijah.

"I will show you," God said.

195

天父引領以利亞
來到溪水旁邊，
可是，溪水旁邊沒有食物。
以利亞問：
「我可以吃些甚麼呢？」

God showed Elijah
a little river.
"But what will I eat?"
Elijah asked.
There was no food
at the river.

天父每天都賜給以利亞食物。
天父差派小鳥送食物
給以利亞。
這樣，以利亞便有好吃的食物，
都是天父每天賜給他的。
以利亞說：「謝謝祢！謝謝祢
把好吃的食物賜給我。」

So God gave Elijah food each day.
He sent birds with food for Elijah.
Now Elijah had good food to eat.
God gave it to him each day.
"Thank you," Elijah said.
"Thank you for giving me good food to eat."

問答題 Something to Ask

1. 天父怎樣把食物賜給以利亞?

2. 天父怎樣把食物賜給你?

3. 你有沒有感謝天父賜給你
   好吃的食物?

4. 你想現在就感謝祂嗎?

1. How did God give food to Elijah?

2. How does God give food to you?

3. Do you thank Him for your good food?

4. Will you thank Him now?

思考題 Something to Do

天父賜給你哪些食物？

What food does God give you?

以利亞幫助一個家庭

以利亞和寡婦・列王紀上 17

很久沒有下雨了，
糧食都不能夠生長，
人們都沒有足夠的食物。
以利亞問：「我到哪裡才能
找到食物呢？」
天父說：「我會指引你。」

Elijah Helps a Family

Elijah and a Widow · 1 Kings 17

No one had much food to eat.

There had been no rain for a long time.

So the food could not grow.

"Where will I get something to eat?" Elijah asked.

"I will show you," God said.

天父告訴以利亞，
到遠處的一個小鎮去。
祂說：「你會在那裡找到一個婦人，
我會給她好吃的食物，
她會分一些給你。」
以利亞走到那個小鎮，
找到那個婦人。
可是，那個婦人却沒有吃的東西，
她問：「到哪裡才能找到我們吃的食物呢？」
以利亞說：「天父會賜給妳。」

God told Elijah where to go.

It was a little town far away.

"You will find a woman there," God said.

"I will give her good food, and she will

give some to you."

Elijah went to the little town.

He found the woman.

But the woman had no food.

"Where will I get food for us?" she asked.

"God will give it to you," said Elijah.

天父果然賜給那個婦人
一些食物帶回家。
天父還把以利亞的食物交給她。
她很高興以利亞來找她。
她說：「你幫助了我們
得到好吃的食物。」
以利亞說：「妳也讓我
有東西吃了。」

God DID give the woman some
food for her family.
He gave her food for Elijah, too.
She was happy that Elijah came.
"You have helped us get good
food," the woman said.
"And you have helped me have
food, too," said Elijah.

問答題 Something to Ask

1. 媽媽和爸爸在哪裡取得你的食物？

2. 你吃的糧食是誰種的？

3. 你能夠種糧食嗎？

4. 你有沒有感謝天父的幫助？

5. 你想現在感謝祂嗎？

1. Where do mother and father get your food?

2. Who makes your food grow?

3. Can you make it grow?

4. Do you thank God for His help?

5. Will you thank Him now?

思考題 Something to Do

天父怎樣幫助你得到食物？

How is God helping you get food?

新蓋的房間

以利沙和書念地方的婦人 · 列王紀下 4

一對夫婦向以利沙說：
「因為你要事奉天父，我們很想
幫助你，請你隨時到我們的家，
和我們一起吃飯。」
這對夫婦不能像以利沙一樣事奉天父。
但是，他們可以供給以利沙食物，讓他能夠專心
事奉天父。以利沙很高興和他們一起吃飯，
他知道他們和他一樣的愛天父。

A New Room

Elisha and the Woman from Shunem · 2 Kings 4

"Please eat with us when you come this way,"
a man and woman told Elisha.
"You work for God. So we want to help you."
The man and woman could not work for God
the way Elisha did.
But they could give him something to eat.
They could help Elisha do God's work.
Elisha was happy to eat with them.
He knew they loved God as much as he did.

有一天，主婦給了以利沙
一個驚喜。
她說：「跟隨我來。」
她帶以利沙來到一個美好的房間。
她說：「這房間是
我們給你新蓋的，
請你隨時到這裡來住宿。」

One day the woman had
a surprise for Elisha.
"Come with me," she said.
She took Elisha to a
beautiful room.
"We made this room for you,"
she said.
"Please stay here when you
come this way."

214

以利沙看到這個
美好的房間，微笑著說：
「謝謝妳為我預備了
這美好的房間！」
主婦說：「我們很高興你
事奉天父，
我們很樂意幫助
你去事奉天父。」

Elisha smiled as he looked at the room.
It was a beautiful place.
"Thank you," said Elisha.
"You put good things in the room for me."
"We are happy that you work for God,"
said the woman.
"And we are happy that we can help you
work for God."

問答題 Something to Ask

1. 誰人事奉天父？

2. 誰幫助以利沙去事奉天父？

3. 他們怎樣幫助他去事奉天父？

1. Who worked for God?

2. Who helped Elisha work for God?

3. How did they help him work for God?

思考題 Something to Do

你可以用分享來事奉天父。

圖中哪些是分享的行為?

You can help do God's work by sharing.

Which of these are ways to do this?

天父幫助生病的人

乃縵和以利沙‧列王紀下 5

乃縵生了重病，他長了大痲瘋，
他想找以利沙來幫助他。
乃縵和他的朋友一起去找以利沙。
以利沙對乃縵的朋友說話，
他沒有對乃縵說話。
他對乃縵的朋友說：
「告訴乃縵到河裡洗澡。」

God Helps a Sick Man

Naaman and Elisha · 2 Kings 5

Naaman went to see Elisha.

A friend went with him.

Naaman was very sick. He had leprosy.

Naaman wanted Elisha to help him.

Elisha talked to Naaman's friend.

He did not talk to Naaman.

"Tell Naaman to wash in the river,"

Elisha told Naaman's friend.

乃縵發怒了，
因為他想見以利沙，
他希望以利沙看重這件事。
他不想在以利沙的河裡洗澡。
這樣，乃縵便離開了。
乃縵的朋友說：「不要離開！
聽以利沙的話去做。」

Naaman was angry.

He wanted to see Elisha.

He wanted Elisha to do something big.

He did not want to wash in Elisha's river.

So Naaman went away.

"Stop!" said Naaman's friend.

"Do what Elisha says."

乃縵跑回來，
他在以利沙的河裡洗澡。
你知道發生了甚麼事嗎？
天父把乃縵的病治好了！
因為乃縵聽從以利沙的話，
所以他身上的大痲瘋
全都消失了。

So Naaman went back.
He washed in Elisha's river.
And what do you think
happened?
God made Naaman well again!
His leprosy went away because
he did what Elisha said.

問答題 Something to Ask

1. 誰生病了？他生了甚麼病？

2. 以利沙告訴他去做些甚麼？

3. 乃縵為甚麼發怒？

4. 乃縵聽從了以利沙的話，
   後來發生了甚麼事？

1. Who was sick? What sickness did he have?

2. What did Elisha tell him to do?

3. Why was Naaman angry?

4. What happened when Naaman obeyed Elisha?

思考題 Something to Do

你應該聽從誰的話？

Who should you obey?

認新詞　　words to know

約阿施　Joash
修建　　Fix
箱子　　Box
金錢　　Money

奉獻修建天父的家

約阿施和錢箱 · 歷代志下 24

約阿施王愛天父。

他希望百姓也愛天父。

他希望百姓到天父的家去，

可是，天父的家再不是一個充滿歡樂的地方。

因為百姓沒有好好的照顧它。

國王說：「我們一定要把天父的家修建好，

可是，我們需要金錢來做這件事。」

Money to Fix God's House

Joash and the Money-Chest · 2 Chronicles 24

King Joash loved God.

He wanted his people to love God, too.

He wanted his people to go to God's house.

But God's house was not

the happy house it should be.

People did not take good care of it.

"We must fix God's house," said the king.

"But we must have money to do that."

國王在天父的家門前放了一個大箱子，
他說：「把你們的金錢放進這箱子裡，
這些金錢是用來修建天父的家。」
百姓把金錢放進那箱子裡，
很快的，國王便有金錢來修建天父的家了。

The king put a big box by God's house.
"Put your money in the box," said the king.
"Put money in there to fix God's house."
The people put their money in the box.
Soon the king had the money to fix God's house.

229

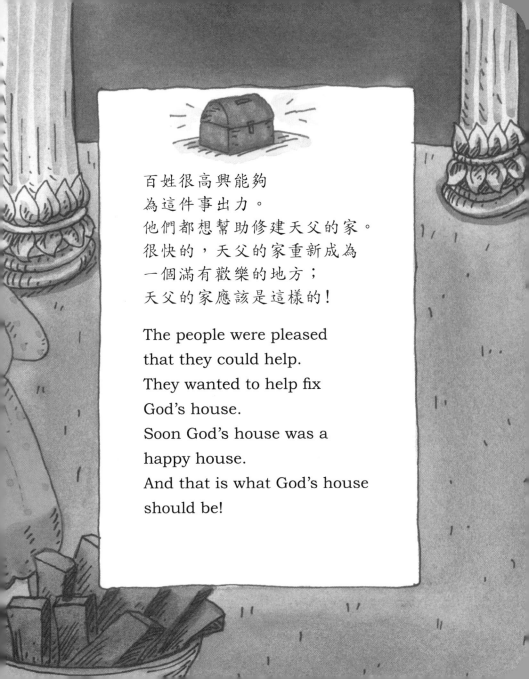

百姓很高興能夠
為這件事出力。
他們都想幫助修建天父的家。
很快的，天父的家重新成為
一個滿有歡樂的地方；
天父的家應該是這樣的！

The people were pleased
that they could help.
They wanted to help fix
God's house.
Soon God's house was a
happy house.
And that is what God's house
should be!

問答題 Something to Ask

1. 約阿施王希望他的百姓做些甚麼？

2. 他們為甚麼做不來？

3. 約阿施王做了些甚麼來幫助天父的家？

1. What did Joash want his people to do?
2. Why couldn't they do it?
3. What did Joash do to help God's house?

思考題 Something to Do

我在天父的家能幫忙些甚麼呢?

How can I help in God's house?

建造新城牆

尼希米在耶路撒冷 · 尼希米記 1-8

尼希米替國王工作。

有一天，尼希米看來很憂傷。

國王問：「你為甚麼這樣憂傷？」

尼希米說：「很久以前，我家鄉的城鎮

被人毀掉了，他們把城牆也拆毀了。」

國王問：「你想我怎樣做呢？」

尼希米說：「請讓我回家把城牆重新再建造。」

國王說：「你回去吧！」

Building New Walls

Nehemiah in Jerusalem · Nehemiah 1-8

Nehemiah worked for the king.

But one day Nehemiah looked sad.

"Why are you so sad?" the king asked.

"Long ago people tore down my city,"

Nehemiah said. "They tore down the walls."

"What do you want me to do?" the king asked.

"Please let me go home," said Nehemiah.

"Please let me build the walls again."

"You may go," said the king.

這樣，尼希米便回到他的家鄉。
他找來一些助手，
他們開始重建城牆。
可是，有些人不喜歡這件事。
他們想傷害尼希米和他的助手。
他們不想尼希米家鄉的城鎮有城牆。

So Nehemiah went home.
He found some helpers.
They began to build the walls.
But some people did not like this.
They wanted to hurt Nehemiah.
They wanted to hurt his helpers.
They did not want Nehemiah's city
to have walls.

237

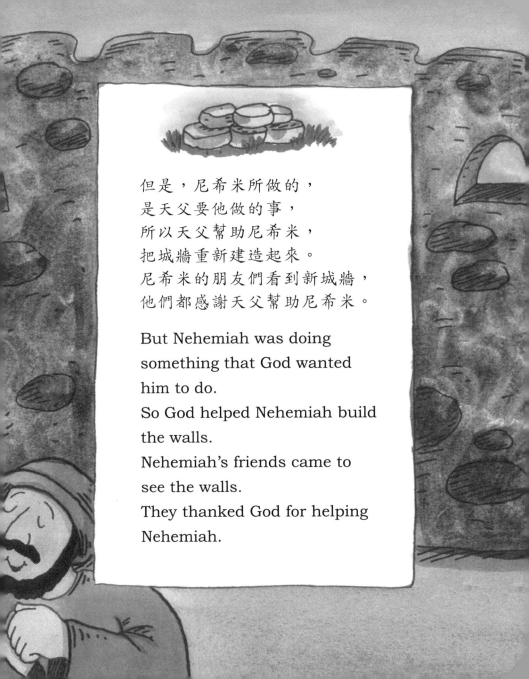

但是，尼希米所做的，
是天父要他做的事，
所以天父幫助尼希米，
把城牆重新建造起來。
尼希米的朋友們看到新城牆，
他們都感謝天父幫助尼希米。

But Nehemiah was doing
something that God wanted
him to do.
So God helped Nehemiah build
the walls.
Nehemiah's friends came to
see the walls.
They thanked God for helping
Nehemiah.

問答題 Something to Ask

1. 尼希米為甚麼感到憂傷？

2. 他想做些甚麼？

3. 國王對他說甚麼？

4. 尼希米的族人為甚麼要感謝天父？

1. Why was Nehemiah sad?

2. What did he want to do?

3. What did the king tell him to do?

4. Why did Nehemiah's people thank God?

思考題 Something to Do

請爸媽幫你忙，找一些小孩子幫忙做家務的圖畫。

Find pictures of boys or girls who are helpers.

Ask mother or father to help you.

圖中的人正在做甚麼？ What are they doing?

你也會做嗎？ Can you do these things, too?

以斯帖是一位勇敢的王后

以斯帖救她的族人 · 以斯帖記 1-10

一個男子走來見以斯帖王后，
他說：「有人想殺害我們的族人。」
王后說：「我可以做些甚麼？」
男子說：「求國王幫助我們。」
可是，以斯帖不能夠這樣做，
她不能隨時去見國王。

Esther Is a
Brave Queen

Esther Saves Her People · Esther 1-10

A man came to see Queen Esther.

"Someone wants to kill our people,"

the man said.

"What can I do?" asked Queen Esther.

"Ask the king to help us," said the man.

But Esther could not do this.

She could not see the king

any time she wanted to see him.

以斯帖說：「要等到國王召見，
我才可以見到他；不然，我會被殺死。」
以斯帖不想被殺死，可是，她愛她的族人。
她終於去見國王。
國王並沒有殺以斯帖。
他對她說能夠為她做些甚麼。
以斯帖王后說：「請幫助我的族人，
有壞人想殺害他們，還想殺害我。」

"The king must ask me to see him,"
said Esther. "I could be killed."
Esther did not want to be killed.
But Esther loved her people.
So she went to see the king.
The king did not kill Esther.
He asked what he could do for her.
"Please help my people," said Queen Esther.
"A bad man wants to kill them.
He will kill me, too."

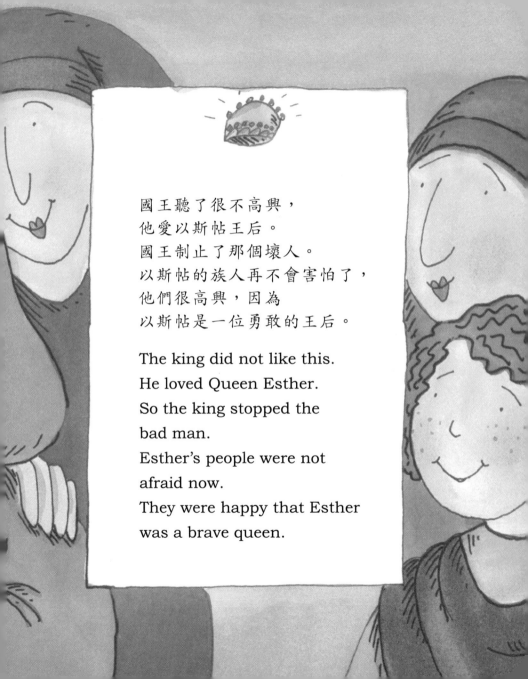

國王聽了很不高興，
他愛以斯帖王后。
國王制止了那個壞人。
以斯帖的族人再不會害怕了，
他們很高興，因為
以斯帖是一位勇敢的王后。

The king did not like this.
He loved Queen Esther.
So the king stopped the
bad man.
Esther's people were not
afraid now.
They were happy that Esther
was a brave queen.

問答題 Something to Ask

1. 以斯帖做了哪些勇敢的事?

2. 她為甚麼要這樣做?

3. 是誰增加以斯帖的勇氣?

4. 天父怎樣幫助你增加勇氣?

1. What did Esther do that was brave?

2. Why did she do this?

3. Who helped Esther to be brave?

4. How can God help you to be brave?

思考題 Something to Do

誰能夠幫助你增加勇氣?

Who can help you to be brave?

耶穌? Jesus?

媽媽? Mother?

爸爸? Father?

朋友們? Friends?

受到傷害的時候要愛天父

約伯受苦難 · 約伯記 1, 42

約伯是一個好人，他愛天父。

天父賜給他很多美好的東西。

有一天，悲傷的事情發生在約伯身上。

有人跑來對他說：「約伯！約伯！

你的一些牲畜被壞人搶走了。」

跟著有人跑來對他說：

「剩下的牲畜都被人殺死了！

連你所有的僕人都被殺死了。」

Love God When You Hurt

Job's Suffering · Job 1, 42

Job was a good man who loved God.

So God gave him many good things.

One day something sad happened to Job.

A man ran up to him and said, "Job! Job!

Bad people took away some of your animals."

Then another man ran up to Job.

"Some of your other animals were killed," he said.

"And your helpers were killed, too."

251

後來，有人跑來對約伯說：
「你的兒女都給人殺死了！」
約伯聽了非常悲傷。
他說：「天父賜給我這些東西，
祂現在都拿走了，這些東西本來
就是屬於天父的。」
後來，約伯病倒了。
這些都是撒但所做的事，祂想傷害約伯，
祂想約伯背棄天父。

Then another man ran up to Job.
"Your children were all killed," he said.
Job was so sad.
"God gave me these things," Job said.
"Then God took them from me.
But they belonged to God."
Then Job became sick.
Satan was doing all these to hurt Job.
He wanted Job to turn away from God.

253

但是，約伯沒有背棄天父。
他說：「我會時刻的愛天父。」
天父也愛約伯，
祂叫撒但不要再傷害約伯。
天父把約伯治好了，
祂賜給他一個新家庭，
還賜給他很多其他的東西。

But Job would not turn away
from God. He said,
"I will love God at all times."
God loved Job, too. He told
Satan to stop hurting Job.
God made Job well again.
He gave him a new family. And He
gave him many other things, too.

問答題 Something to Ask

1. 撒但對約伯做了些甚麼?

2. 約伯感到悲傷嗎? 他受到傷害嗎?

3. 約伯有沒有背棄天父?

4. 當你受到傷害時,你會怎樣做?

5. 天父會幫助你嗎?

1. What did Satan do to Job?

2. Was Job sad? Did Job hurt?

3. Did Job turn away from God?

4. What do you do when you hurt?

5. Will God help you then?

思考題 Something to Do

以下哪些事情會讓你感到受傷害？

當你不能把事情做好？

當朋友們說你的壞話？

當爸媽不在你身邊？

當你生病的時候？

當其他人不喜歡你？

當你需要得到幫助的時候？

Which of these will make you hurt?

When you cannot do something well?
When friends say bad things about you?
When mother or father is away?
When you are sick?
When others do not like you?
When you must have help?

你應該怎樣做呢？

What should you do then?

一位快樂的國王

但以理替國王解夢．但以理書 2

國王說：「我做了一個夢，
可是，我不知道它的意思。」
他對臣子們說：「告訴我夢裡的意思，
和將有甚麼事情要發生。」
臣子們說：「我們怎麼知道你夢裡的意思？」
國王說：「如果你們不能把夢裡的意思告訴我，
我會派人把你們殺死！」
臣子們都很害怕。

A Happy King

Daniel Interprets the King's Dream · Daniel 2

"I had a dream," said the king.

"But I do not know what it means."

"Tell me what I dreamed," he said to his men.

"Then tell me what will come from it."

"How can we tell you what you dreamed?"

the men said.

"If you do not tell me my dream," said

the king, "I will have someone kill you."

The king's men were afraid.

259

可是，但以理沒有感到害怕。
他對國王說：「我會告訴你夢裡的意思。」
然後，但以理向天父禱告，
他說：「請祢讓我知道夢裡的意思。」
天父讓但以理明白國王夢裡的意思。
但以理說：「感謝天父！感謝祢給我
講解了國王的夢。」

But Daniel was not afraid.
He said to the king, "I will tell
you about your dream."
Then Daniel talked to God
about the king's dream.
"Help me know what it is," he asked.
So God helped Daniel know
what the king's dream was about.
"Thank you, God," said Daniel. "Thank you
for telling me about the king's dream."

但以理替國王講解了他的夢，
國王很高興知道夢裡的意思。
國王對但以理很好，
他送給但以理很多美好的東西。
但以理非常感謝天父的幫助。

Then Daniel told the king
about his dream.
The king was happy to know
about the dream.
The king was kind to Daniel.
He gave Daniel many good
things.
Then Daniel thanked God
for His help.

問答題 Something to Ask

1. 但以理為甚麼因著國王的夢
   向天父禱告?

2. 天父替但以理做了些甚麼?

3. 你得到了天父的幫助,
   應該對祂說些甚麼?

4. 你想現在就對祂說嗎?

1. Why did Daniel talk to God about the
   king's dream?

2. What did God do for Daniel?

3. What should you say to God when He
   helps you?

4. Will you say it now?

思考題 Something to Do

你會在這些時間去感謝天父嗎?

Do you thank God at these times?

但以理和獅子

天父幫助但以理 · 但以理書 6

有些人說：「國王要任用
但以理來管治我們。」
他們不喜歡這樣，
他們想管治但以理。
他們求國王制定一條壞法例；
法例這樣說：「任何人都不可以向任何神
祈求任何東西，違反的人
要捉去餵獅子。」

Daniel and the Lions

God Helps Daniel · Daniel 6

"The king is going to put Daniel over us,"
some men said. They did not like this.
They wanted to be over Daniel.
So the men asked the king to make a bad rule.
"No one may ask any god for anything,"
the law said. "If he does, he will be
given to the lions to eat."

這些人知道但以理常常向天父禱告。
他們知道他會求天父的幫助。
那些監視但以理房子的人，
看見但以理向天父禱告，馬上跑去告訴國王。
國王喜歡但以理，
他不喜歡這些人所做的事。
可是，但以理違反了法例，
國王只好任由這些人，把但以理放進獅子洞裡。
國王說：「願你的天父幫助你！」

These men knew that Daniel talked to God.
They knew that he would ask God for help.
The men watched Daniel's house.
They saw Daniel talking to God.
So the men ran to tell the king.
The king liked Daniel.
He did not like what these men had done.
But the king had to let the men put Daniel
into the lion house. This was the law.
"Your God will help you," the king said.

第二天，國王走到獅子洞口，
他說：「但以理，你的天父
有幫助你嗎？」
但以理說：「有呀！
獅子沒有傷害我。」
國王非常高興！但以理也很高興！
因為天父幫助了他。

The next day the king went
to the lion house.
"Did your God help you,
Daniel?" he asked.
"Yes," said Daniel.
"The lions did not hurt me."
The king was so happy.
Daniel was happy, too.
God had helped him.

問答題 Something to Ask

1. 天父怎樣幫助但以理?

2. 但以理受到傷害時為甚麼
   要向天父禱告?

3. 你為甚麼要禱告?

4. 你是不是每天禱告?

1. How did God help Daniel?

2. Why did Daniel talk to God when
   he hurt?

3. Why do you pray?

4. Do you pray each day?

思考題 Something to Do

在甚麼情況之下你會停止禱告？

What would stop you from praying?

遇見飢餓的獅子？
A hungry lion?

在國王面前？
A king?

和壞人在一起？
Bad people?

看電視的時候？
Watching TV?

273

認新詞 | words to know

約拿 | Jonah
尼尼微 | Nineveh
狂風暴雨 | Storm
吞下 | Swallow
陸地 | Land

約拿學習服從

約拿和魚‧約拿書 1-3

天父吩咐約拿到尼尼微城去，
可是，約拿不願意去，他乘船逃走了。
天父差派狂風暴雨，
吹打約拿乘坐的船。
船上其他的人都很害怕。
約拿對他們說：「是我在逃避天父，
如果你們把我拋到海裡，
天父會叫狂風暴雨停止。」

Jonah Learns to Obey

Jonah and the Fish · Jonah 1-3

God sent a big storm.

Jonah was on a boat in the storm.

God had told Jonah to go to Nineveh.

Jonah did not want to go. So he ran away.

The other people on the boat were afraid.

Jonah said, "I am running away from God.

If you throw me into the water,

God will stop the storm."

275

那些人把約拿拋進海裡，
狂風暴雨真的停止了。
跟著，天父差派一條大魚，
天父要牠把約拿吞進肚子裡；
大魚真的把約拿吞了。
約拿在魚腹裡過了一段很長的時間。
約拿在魚腹裡向天父禱告，
他對天父說他後悔了，請求天父饒恕他。

The men threw Jonah into the water.

The storm stopped.

Then God sent a big fish.

God told the fish to swallow Jonah.

The big fish swallowed Jonah.

Jonah was in the fish for a long time.

There in the fish, Jonah prayed to God.

He told God he was sorry.

He asked God to forgive him.

天父對大魚說：「讓約拿離開吧！」
大魚服從天父，
牠把約拿吐在陸地上。
天父重新吩咐約拿到尼尼微城去。
這一次，約拿服從天父。
他到尼尼微城去，
告訴人們關於天父的事。

Then God told the fish,
"Let Jonah go."
The fish obeyed God.
It threw Jonah out on the land.
Then God told Jonah to go to
Nineveh again.
This time Jonah obeyed.
He went and told the people
of Nineveh about God.

問答題 Something to Ask

1. 約拿為甚麼要逃避天父？

2. 天父在哪裡找到他？

3. 天父做了些甚麼？

4. 約拿後來為甚麼到尼尼微城去？

1. Why did Jonah run away from God?

2. Where did God find him?

3. What did God do?

4. Why did Jonah go to Nineveh then?

思考題 Something to Do

下面哪些文字指出約拿在魚腹中所做的事?
Which words tell what Jonah did in the fish?

禱告	後悔	發怒	打架	饒恕
pray	sorry	angry	fight	forgive

耶穌降生是為了愛我們

基督降生・路加福音 2, 馬太福音 1

店主人說：「你們不能在這裡住宿，
因為客房已經住滿了。」
約瑟問：「我們可以睡在哪裡呢?
馬利亞快要生孩子了。」
店主人看著他的牲畜說：
「你們可以睡在牠們的地方，
我只剩下這個地方了。」
馬利亞和約瑟只好睡在牲畜居住的地方。

Jesus Came to Love Us

Christ Is Born · Luke 2, Matthew 1

"You cannot stay here," the man said.

"I have all the people I can take."

"But where can we sleep?" Joseph asked.

"Mary is going to have a Baby."

The man looked at his animals.

"You may sleep with them," he said.

"It is the only place I have."

So Mary and Joseph went to sleep with the animals.

283

當天晚上，
馬利亞誕下了一個小嬰孩。
約瑟說：「我們要稱祂耶穌，
是天父吩咐我們
這樣做的。」

That night Mary had a
little Baby.
"We will call Him Jesus,"
Joseph said.
"That is what God said
we should do."

馬利亞說：「天父說這小嬰孩
是祂的兒子。」
馬利亞和約瑟一起說：
「這小嬰孩是為了愛我們而降生的，
祂來幫助我們去愛天父。」

"This Baby is God's Son," said Mary.

"That is what God said."

"This Baby has come to love us,"

said Mary and Joseph.

"And He has come to help us love God."

問答題 Something to Ask

1. 這小嬰孩是誰?

2. 祂為甚麼要降生?

3. 耶穌愛你嗎?

4. 你愛耶穌嗎?

1. Who was this little Baby?

2. Why did He come?

3. Does Jesus love you?

4. Do you love Jesus?

思考題 Something to Do

你怎樣向耶穌表示你愛祂呢?

How do you show Jesus that you love Him?

天使們給牧羊人唱歌

牧羊人尋訪聖嬰耶穌・路加福音 2

一個牧羊人說：「看看天空。」
另一個牧羊人說：「現在是晚上，
可是，天空看來像白天一樣。」
牧羊人都很害怕，
他們不知道為甚麼會這樣。

Angels Sing to Shepherds

The Shepherds Visit Baby Jesus · Luke 2

"Look at the sky," a shepherd said.

"It looks like it is day," said another.

"But it is night."

The shepherds were so afraid.

They did not know what it was.

一個天使說：「不要害怕，
讓我告訴你們一件事：
你們要到城裡去，探望一個
剛誕生的嬰孩，
祂是天父的兒子。」
跟著，更多的天使飛過來，
擠滿了天空。
天使們歌頌天父，然後便離去。

"Don't be afraid," an angel said.
"I have something to tell you.
There is a new Baby in town.
You should go to see Him.
He is God's Son." Then more
angels came and filled the sky.
They sang about God.
Then they went away.

牧羊人說：「讓我們進城去看聖嬰，
祂是天父的兒子。」
他們進了城，來到天使告訴他們要去的地方。
他們很高興親眼看到聖嬰耶穌！
他們要告訴其他的人
關於天父兒子的事。
牧羊人把這件事告訴了所有他們遇見的人。

"Let's go into town
and see the Baby who is God's Son,"
the shepherds said.
They ran into town and went where
the angels said they should go.
How happy they were that they
could see Baby Jesus!
They wanted to tell others about God's Son.
The shepherds told all the people they could find
about God's Son.

問答題 Something to Ask

1. 牧羊人看見了誰?

2. 天使把哪些關於耶穌的事
   告訴牧羊人?

3. 牧羊人把哪些事告訴其他的人?

4. 你會把耶穌的事告訴你的朋友嗎?

5. 你會告訴他們些甚麼?

1. Who did the shepherds see?

2. What did the angels tell the shepherds
   about Jesus?

3. What did the shepherds tell others?

4. Do you tell your friends about Jesus?

5. What do you tell them?

思考題 Something to Do

你會告訴其他人哪些和耶穌有關的事?
　　祂愛我們。
　　祂是我的朋友。
　　祂也要和你做朋友。
　　祂要你為祂活著。
　　祂會幫助你將來能夠住在天上天父的家。

你還要講述其他有關耶穌的事嗎?

What do you tell others about Jesus?
　　He loves us.
　　He is my friend.
　　He wants to be your friend, too.
　　He wants you to live for Him.
　　He will help you live in God's home in heaven.

What other things do you tell about Jesus?

認新詞	words to know
跟隨	Follow
不平凡	Special
駱駝	Camels
禮物	Gift
伯利恆	Bethlehem

博士獻上最好的禮物

聖嬰耶穌的禮物・馬太福音 2

一位滿有智慧的博士說：
「看看那顆星。」
另一位說：「我看見了，
我們一定要跟隨那顆星。
它會引領我們找到
那位新生的王。」

The Wise Men Give Their Best

Gifts for Baby Jesus · Matthew 2

"Look at the star," a wise man said.
"I see it," said another.
"We must follow that star.
It will take us to a new King."

博士們知道祂是一位不平凡的王；
祂現在還是小嬰孩，
祂是天父派來的。
博士們騎著駱駝，帶著他們
最好的禮物，送給這位新生的王。
他們跟隨著那顆星。
他們走了一段很長的日子。

The wise men knew that
this King was a special King.
He was only a little Baby now.
But God had sent Him.
The wise men went on camels.
They took their best gifts
to give to the Baby King.
On and on they went for many
days, following the star.

有一天，那顆星停在伯利恆城的上空。
博士們說：「就是這個地方。
新生王就在這裡。」
博士們跑過去探望耶穌，
把他們最好的禮物獻給祂。
他們很高興那顆引路的星，
把他們帶到耶穌的跟前來。

One day the star stopped.

It stopped over the town of Bethlehem.

"This is the place," the wise men said.

"The Baby King is here."

The wise men went to see Jesus.

They gave Him their best gifts.

They were happy that the star

had led them to Jesus.

問答題 Something to Ask

1. 給博士們引路的是甚麼?

2. 他們獻甚麼禮物給祂?

3. 你有沒有把最好的禮物獻給耶穌?

1. What led the wise men to Jesus?

2. What did they give Him?

3. Do you give Jesus your best gifts?

思考題 Something to Do

你要把圖中的哪些禮物獻給耶穌?

Which of these gifts can you give Jesus?

耶穌的快樂家庭

耶穌的童年 · 路加福音 2

約瑟說：「祢願意幫助我嗎?」
耶穌當然願意幫助約瑟。
約瑟是一位木匠，
他用木頭造了很多很好的東西。
耶穌也是一位木匠，
祂幫助約瑟把木頭造成有用的東西。

Jesus' Happy Family

The Childhood of Jesus · Luke 2

"Will You help me?" Joseph asked.

Jesus was happy to help Joseph.

Joseph made many good things.

He made things from wood.

Joseph was a carpenter.

Jesus was a carpenter, too.

He helped Joseph make things from wood.

約瑟對馬利亞說：
「看耶穌造了些甚麼？」
馬利亞說：「真好，
耶穌是個好木匠！」
約瑟、馬利亞和耶穌
一家人住在小鎮裡。
他們一起前往小鎮上
天父的家。

"See what Jesus made?"
Joseph said to Mary.
"Yes," said Mary.
"Jesus is a good carpenter."
Joseph and Mary and Jesus
lived in a little town.
They went to God's house
in the little town.

他們都喜歡聽到天父所講的話。
他們都喜歡在那裡向天父禱告。
他們都喜歡和天父的子民說話。
人們都說：「他們有一個快樂的家庭。
他們不單是好木匠，
他們還要替天父做美好的事。」

They liked to hear God's Word.
They liked to talk to God there.
And they liked to talk to God's people.
"They are a happy family," people said.
"They do good work with wood.
And they do good work for God, too."

問答題 Something to Ask

1. 約瑟做的是甚麼工作?

2. 耶穌怎樣幫助他?

3. 好助手可以給家庭帶來快樂嗎?

4. 你是個好助手嗎?

5. 你怎樣幫助你的家庭得到快樂呢?

1. What work did Joseph do?

2. How did Jesus help him?

3. Do good helpers make happy families?

4. Are you a good helper?

5. How can you help your family to be happy?

思考題 Something to Do

圖中哪些情境能表示你有快樂的家庭？哪些情境不能？

Which of these will help your family be happy?

Which will not help your family be happy?

313

耶穌討天父的喜悅

基督受引誘 · 馬太福音 4

耶穌現在是一位男子漢。
有一天，祂離開了祂住的小鎮，
獨自走到曠野，每天向天父禱告。
耶穌已經很久沒有吃東西了。
撒但走來見耶穌，想引誘祂。
祂說：「祢可以把那些石頭變成食物。」

認新詞　words to know

長大　Grew
獨自　Alone
石頭　Rock
引誘　Tempt
三　　Three

Jesus Pleases God

The Temptation of Christ · Matthew 4

Jesus grew and became a Man.

One day Jesus went away from His town.

He wanted to be alone.

Jesus talked to God for many days.

Then Satan came to see Jesus.

Jesus had not had food for a long time.

"You can make food from those rocks,"

Satan said. He was tempting Jesus.

耶穌知道祂不可以照撒但的話去做。
耶穌說：「我只聽從天父的吩咐。」
撒但一連三次，
要耶穌去做天父不喜悅的事。
但是，耶穌沒有照撒但的話去做。
耶穌對撒但說：
「我一定要討天父的喜悅。」

But Jesus knew that He must not do
what Satan said.
"I must do what God tells Me," said Jesus.
Satan asked Jesus three times to do
something that God would not like.
But Jesus would not do what Satan said.
"I must please God," Jesus told Satan.

317

撒但知道不能叫耶穌
做牠想做的事，
牠終於離開了耶穌。
天父非常喜悅，耶穌
沒有聽從撒但的話去做。

Satan saw that he could
not get Jesus
to do what he wanted.
So Satan went away.
God was very pleased.
Jesus would not do what
Satan said.

問答題 Something to Ask

1. 撒但想要耶穌做些甚麼?

2. 耶穌怎樣做?

3. 撒但想你去做些甚麼?

4. 你應該怎樣做?

1. What did Satan want Jesus to do?

2. But what did Jesus do?

3. What kinds of things does Satan want you to do?

4. What should you do?

思考題 Something to Do

當你受到引誘，想做壞事的時候，你應該怎樣做？

What should you do when you are tempted
to do bad things?

想做就去做？
Do what you want?

找朋友幫助你？
Ask a friend to help you?

求天父幫助你？
Ask God to help you?

請爸媽幫助你？
Ask mother or
father to help you?

天父的家

耶穌趕走換銀錢的人 · 約翰福音 2

耶穌喜歡來到天父的家。

祂喜歡在那裡向天父禱告。

祂喜歡和天父的子民在一起。

但是，耶穌不喜歡有些人所做的事，

他們不是向天父禱告，

他們也不是和天父的子民說話，

他們在天父的家賣牛、羊和鴿子。

God's House

Jesus Drives Out the Money-Changers · John 2

Jesus liked to go to God's house.

He liked to talk to God there.

He liked to be with God's people.

But Jesus did not like

what some men were doing.

They were not talking with God.

They were not talking with God's people.

These men sold animals in God's house.

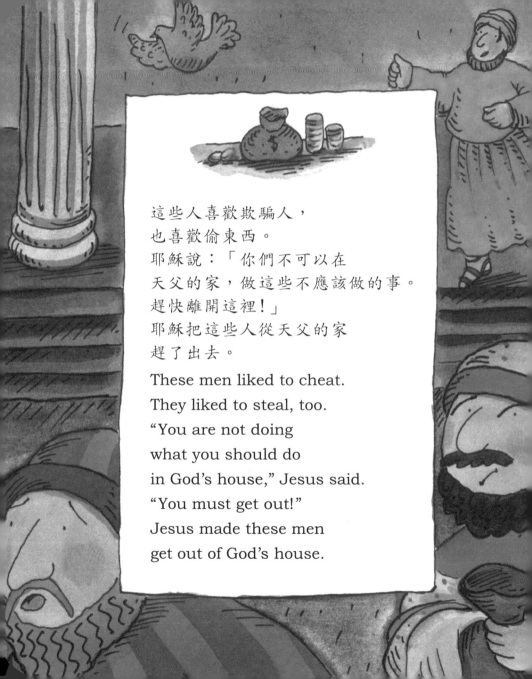

這些人喜歡欺騙人，
也喜歡偷東西。
耶穌說：「你們不可以在
天父的家，做這些不應該做的事。
趕快離開這裡！」
耶穌把這些人從天父的家
趕了出去。

These men liked to cheat.
They liked to steal, too.
"You are not doing
what you should do
in God's house," Jesus said.
"You must get out!"
Jesus made these men
get out of God's house.

耶穌說：「不可以在天父的家
欺騙人和偷東西。
我們到天父的家和祂在一起。
我們應該在天父的家向祂禱告。
我們也應該和天父的子民說話。」

"God's house is not a place to cheat
and steal," said Jesus.
"We should go to God's house to
be with Him.
We should talk to God in His house.
We should talk with God's people, too."

問答題 Something to Ask

1. 人們在天父的家應該做些甚麼？

2. 有些人在天父的家做了些甚麼？

3. 耶穌叫他們做些甚麼？

4. 你在天父的家會做些甚麼？

5. 你應該要做些甚麼？

1. What should people do in God's house?

2. What were the men doing there?

3. What did Jesus tell them to do?

4. What do YOU do when you go to God's house?

5. What should you do?

思考題 Something to Do

你在天父的家會找到哪些人？

天父？
天父的朋友？
你那些愛天父的朋友？
其他愛天父的人？

Who will you find in God's house?

God?
God's friends?
Your friends who love God?
Others who love God?

我在天父的家應該做甚麼？

耶穌讀經 · 路加福音 4

有些人說：「看看誰來了！」
所有的人都看著耶穌走進來。
耶穌走進了天父的家。
祂走到人們能夠看見祂的地方，
然後，祂打開了聖經。

What Should I Do in God's House?

Jesus Reads from the Scriptures · Luke 4

"Look who is here!" some people said.

All the people looked. Jesus was coming.

He was coming into God's house.

Jesus went up where the people could see Him.

Then He looked at God's Word.

耶穌開始讀經文。

男孩子和女孩子都很安靜。

爸爸、媽媽也很安靜。

耶穌告訴他們關於天父兒子的事；

還說經文上有提到祂的事。

祂告訴人們，說：「我是天父的兒子。」

但有些人說：

「不，祢不是天父的兒子。」

Jesus began to read what God's Word said.

The boys and girls were quiet.

The mothers and fathers were quiet, too.

Jesus told them about God's Son.

He told them what God's Word said about Him.

"I am God's Son," He told them.

"No," some of the people said.

"You are not God's Son."

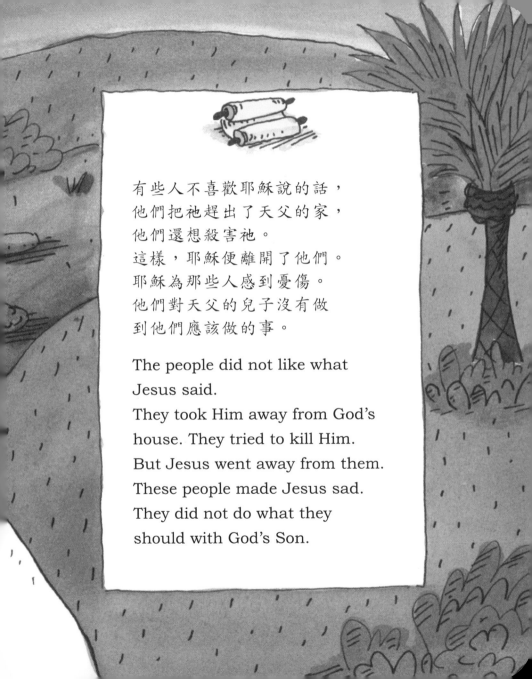

有些人不喜歡耶穌說的話，
他們把祂趕出了天父的家，
他們還想殺害祂。
這樣，耶穌便離開了他們。
耶穌為那些人感到憂傷。
他們對天父的兒子沒有做
到他們應該做的事。

The people did not like what
Jesus said.
They took Him away from God's
house. They tried to kill Him.
But Jesus went away from them.
These people made Jesus sad.
They did not do what they
should with God's Son.

問答題 Something to Ask

1. 耶穌在天父的家做了些甚麼？

2. 人們做了些甚麼？

3. 人們在天父的家，應該怎樣看待天父的兒子？

1. What did Jesus do in God's house?

2. What did the people do?

3. What should people do with God's Son in God's house?

思考題 Something to Do

你在天父的家應該做甚麼？

What things should you do in God's house?

一個生病的朋友

耶穌治好癱子 · 馬可福音 2

有些人問：「耶穌在房子裡嗎？」
其他的人說：「是的，但房子裡的人太多了，
你們沒法走進來。」
那些人說：「我們的朋友生病了，
耶穌能夠把他治好。」
可是，他們沒法走進房子裡。

A Friend Who Was Sick

Jesus Heals a Paralytic · Mark 2

"Is Jesus in the house?" some men asked.

"Yes, but you cannot get in," said others.

"There are too many people."

"Our friend is sick," said the men,

"and Jesus can make him well."

But the men could not get into the house.

房子裡到處擠滿了人，
他們實在不能走進去。
他們說：「我們從另外的地方進
去吧。」跟著，他們把那個
生病的朋友，從房頂吊下去；
他們對耶穌說：
「請幫助我們那生病的朋友。」

There were people here and
people there.
The men could not get through.
"Then we will go in another
way," they said.
So they let their friend down
through the roof.
"Please help our friend," they
said to Jesus. "He is sick."

耶穌很樂意幫助他們那個生病的朋友。
耶穌對他說：「起來，你的病好了。」
那個人立刻站起來，他現在沒有病了。
他非常快樂。他對耶穌說：
「謝謝祢！謝謝祢！」
他們都很快樂，
因為他們那個朋友的病好了，
是耶穌把他治好的。

Jesus was happy to help their sick friend.

"Get up," said Jesus. "You are well."

The man got up. He was not sick now.

He was so happy.

"Thank you! Thank you!" he said.

The men were happy, too.

Their friend did not hurt now.

Jesus had made him well.

問答題 Something to Ask

1. 病人的朋友做了些甚麼?

2. 耶穌怎樣幫助他們?

3. 你受到傷害時,耶穌怎樣幫助你?

4. 你會不會求祂幫助你?

1. What did the sick man's friends do?

2. How did Jesus help?

3. How can Jesus help you when you hurt?

4. Will you ask Him to help you?

思考題 Something to Do

朋友受到傷害的時候，你會用哪些方法來幫助他？

求天父幫助他？

告訴他你是他的朋友？

請別人來幫助他？

對他說他的情況很壞？

告訴他你是多麼的好？

What can you do for a friend when he hurts?

Which of these would you do?

Ask God to help him?

Tell him you are his friend? Ask others to help him?

Tell him how bad he is? Tell him how good you are?

事奉天父
耶穌呼召馬太 · 馬太福音 9

馬太有一份很好的工作。

他有很多錢財。

人們都要聽從他的吩咐去做。

可是，馬太並不快樂，

他知道天父不喜歡他所做的工作。

Doing God's Work
Jesus Calls Matthew · Matthew 9

Matthew had good work.

He had all the money he wanted.

And people did what he told them to do.

But Matthew was not happy.

He knew that he did not please God in his work.

347

有一天，耶穌來看馬太。
耶穌說：「馬太，
跟從我，和我一起工作吧！」
馬太看著耶穌。
他知道耶穌不會支付他的工錢，
他也不能再賺到很多金錢。
人們不會再聽從他的吩咐去做。
他必須聽從耶穌的話去做。
馬太問：「我該怎樣做呢？」

One day Jesus came to see Matthew.
"Matthew," Jesus said,
"come with Me and work for Me."
Matthew looked at Jesus.
Jesus would not pay him for his work.
He would not make much money.
People would not do what he said.
He would have to do what Jesus said.
"What should I do?" Matthew asked.

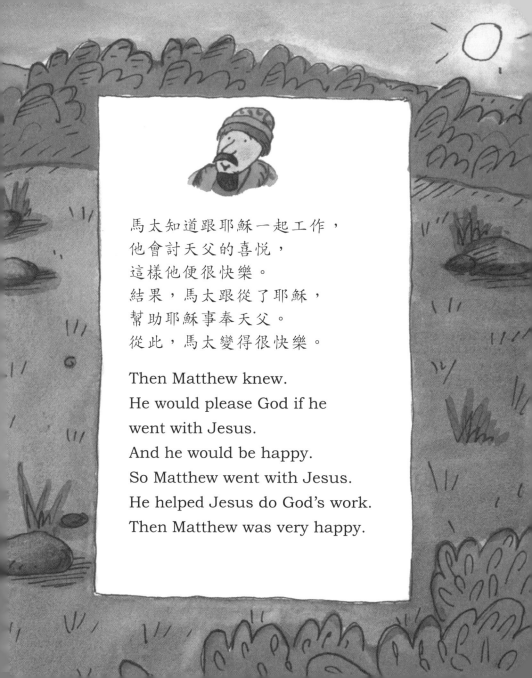

馬太知道跟耶穌一起工作，
他會討天父的喜悅，
這樣他便很快樂。
結果，馬太跟從了耶穌，
幫助耶穌事奉天父。
從此，馬太變得很快樂。

Then Matthew knew.
He would please God if he
went with Jesus.
And he would be happy.
So Matthew went with Jesus.
He helped Jesus do God's work.
Then Matthew was very happy.

問答題 Something to Ask

1. 馬太為甚麼不快樂?

2. 怎樣才能叫馬太變得快樂?

3. 怎樣才能叫你得到快樂?

4. 你會這樣做嗎?

1. Why was Matthew not happy?

2. What helped him become happy?

3. What can make YOU happy?

4. Will you do these things?

思考題 Something to Do

怎樣才能叫你得到快樂？

做天父要你做的事？　做朋友們告訴你要做的事？

做爸爸、媽媽吩咐你做的事？　做你自己想要做的事？

What will make you happy:

When you do what God wants?
When you do what your friends tell you to do?
When you do what mother and father ask you?
When you do what you want?

看耶穌的大能

耶穌止住了風浪 · 路加福音 8

耶穌說：「跟隨我來。」

祂的朋友們問：「到哪裡去?」

耶穌說：「到湖的對岸去。」

耶穌和朋友們上了船。

他們喜歡跟耶穌在一起。

他們知道耶穌替天父做美好的事。

他們知道天父幫助耶穌做這些事。

Look What Jesus Can Do!

Jesus Stills a Storm · Luke 8

"Come with Me," said Jesus.

"Where?" asked His friends.

"To the other side of the lake," Jesus said.

Jesus and His friends got into their boat.

These friends liked to go with Jesus.

They knew that Jesus did good things for God.

They knew that God helped Jesus do these things.

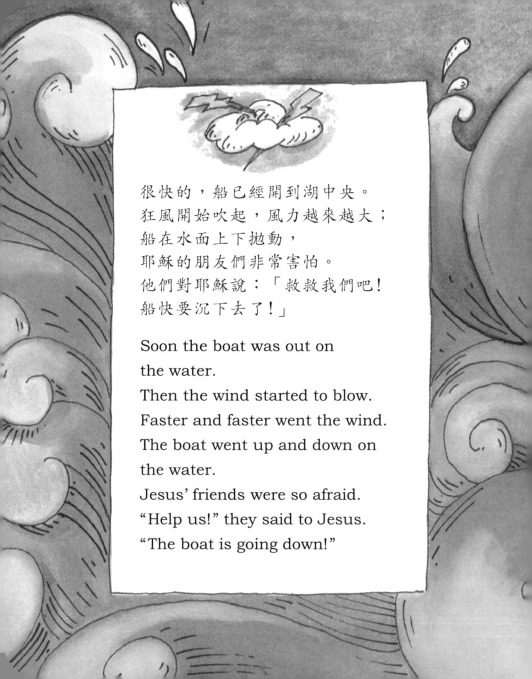

很快的，船已經開到湖中央。
狂風開始吹起，風力越來越大；
船在水面上下拋動，
耶穌的朋友們非常害怕。
他們對耶穌說：「救救我們吧！
船快要沉下去了！」

Soon the boat was out on
the water.
Then the wind started to blow.
Faster and faster went the wind.
The boat went up and down on
the water.
Jesus' friends were so afraid.
"Help us!" they said to Jesus.
"The boat is going down!"

耶穌看著水面上吹起的狂風說：
「靜下來！」
狂風馬上停止了，海浪也靜下來，
船再沒有上下拋動了。
朋友們都看著耶穌，其中的一位說：
「你們都看見吧！」
他們都說：「唯有天父的兒子才能夠這樣做。」

Jesus looked at the wind blowing on the water.

"Stop!" He said.

The wind stopped blowing.

The water stopped going up and down.

And the boat stopped going up and down.

"Did you see that?" one of Jesus' friends said.

The others looked at Jesus.

"Only God's Son could do that," they said.

問答題 Something to Ask

1. 誰人吩咐狂風照祂的話去做？

2. 祂為甚麼能夠這樣做呢？

3. 你知道誰能夠這樣做嗎？

4. 你能夠這樣做嗎？

5. 你有聽從耶穌的吩咐去做嗎？

1. Who told the wind what to do?

2. How could He do that?

3. Do you know anyone who can do that?

4. Can you do that?

5. Do you do what Jesus wants, too?

思考題 Something to Do

圖中所見的，哪些會聽從耶穌的吩咐去做呢？

Which of these should do what Jesus says to do?

人能夠這樣做嗎？

耶穌治好小女孩・馬可福音 5

睚魯說：「我的小女兒快要死了，
請祢趕快到我家。」
耶穌和睚魯一起走，
可是，他們要走一段很遠的路，
才能到達睚魯的家。
路上到處都擠滿了人，
他們都想來看耶穌。

Can a Man Do This?

Jesus Heals a Little Girl · Mark 5

"Please come to my house," Jairus said.

"My little girl is going to die."

Jesus went with Jairus.

But it took a long time to get to his house.

People were here.

People were there.

The people all wanted to see Jesus.

有人從睚魯的家跑出來，說：
「你的小女兒已經死了。」
睚魯聽了很傷心。耶穌說：
「不用怕。」他們走進房子裡，
看見很多人在哭泣。
耶穌說：「小女孩睡著了，
不用傷心。」

Then someone came from
Jairus' house and said,
"Your little girl has died."
Jairus was so sad, but Jesus
said, "Don't be afraid."
Jesus and Jairus went into the
house. People were crying.
"Don't be sad," said Jesus.
"The little girl is sleeping."

有些人取笑耶穌。

耶穌對他們說：「離開這房子吧！」

這樣，那些取笑祂的人都離開了。

耶穌看著小女孩，對她說：

「小女孩，起來吧！」小女孩便起來了。

耶穌說：「給她吃一點東西吧。」

睚魯和小女孩的媽媽都很快樂。

他們都說：「人能夠這樣做嗎？

耶穌一定是天父的兒子！」

Some people laughed at Jesus.

"Get out of this house," Jesus said to them.

So the people who laughed went away.

Jesus looked at the girl.

"Get up, little girl!" He said to her.

The little girl got up.

"Give her something to eat," said Jesus.

Jairus and the girl's mother were so happy.

"Can a man do this?" they asked.

"Jesus must be God's Son!"

問答題 Something to Ask

1. 耶穌為小女孩做了些甚麼?

2. 人能夠這樣做嗎?

3. 誰是耶穌?

4. 甚麼書能告訴你關於耶穌的事?

1. What did Jesus do for the girl?

2. Can a man do this?

3. Who is Jesus?

4. What book tells you about Jesus?

思考題 Something to Do

圖中哪些人聽從耶穌的吩咐去做?

Which of these people did what Jesus said?

睚魯?
Jairus?

小女孩?
The little girl?

在睚魯家的人?
The people in
Jairus' house?

你自己?
Do you?

小男孩分享他的午餐

耶穌讓五千人吃飽．馬太福音 14

媽媽說：「這五個餅和
兩尾魚是你的午餐。」
小男孩很高興，因為他要和
朋友們一起去看耶穌。
小男孩帶著他的午餐跟朋友們一起跑過去；
他們終於看見了耶穌，
還看到很多其他的人。

A Boy Shares His Lunch

Jesus Feeds the Five Thousand · Matthew 14

"Here are five pieces of bread
and two fish for your lunch," a mother said.

The boy was happy.

He was going to see Jesus.

So were some of his friends.

The boy took his lunch. He ran with his friends.

At last they saw Jesus.

There were many other people there, too.

371

耶穌講了很多美好的教訓。
小男孩和朋友們都用心聆聽。
後來，耶穌停止了說話，有人來到
小男孩的面前，對他說：「耶穌想
要你的午餐，你可以給我們嗎？」
小男孩把他的午餐給了耶穌，
他很樂意把他的午餐給耶穌。

Jesus said many good things.
The boy and his friends listened.
Then Jesus stopped talking.
Some men came to the boy.
"May we have your lunch?"
they asked. "Jesus wants it."
The boy took his lunch to Jesus.
He was happy to give Jesus
his lunch.

小男孩和朋友們都在看，
可是，耶穌沒有吃那午餐。
祂把食物擘開，分成小塊，
再把小塊分給每一個人。
很快的，所有的人都吃飽了。
耶穌微笑著對小男孩和他的
朋友們說：「謝謝你的午餐！」
小男孩也微笑著，
坐在耶穌身旁，吃著餅和魚。

The boy and his friends watched.

But Jesus did not eat the lunch.

He broke it into many pieces.

He gave the pieces to the people.

Soon all the people had as much

to eat as they wanted.

Jesus smiled at the boy and his friends.

"Thank you for your lunch," He said.

The boy smiled, too.

Then he sat near Jesus and ate some bread and fish.

問答題 Something to Ask

1. 小男孩的午餐有些甚麼?

2. 耶穌拿了午餐後做了些甚麼?

3. 小男孩樂意把他的午餐和
   耶穌分享嗎?

4. 你樂意和耶穌分享你的東西嗎?

1. What was in the boy's lunch?

2. What did Jesus do with it?

3. Was the boy happy to share his
   lunch with Jesus?

4. Would you like to share something
   with Jesus?

思考題 Something to Do

有些甚麼你能夠和耶穌來分享？

你可以向爸媽請教這個問題。

What could you share with Jesus?

Talk with mother or father about this.

在水面上行走

耶穌在加利利海面上走．馬可福音 6

認新詞　words to know

猛烈　Hard
忽然　Suddenly
鬼　Ghost

耶穌說：
「現在是你們回家的時候了。」
祂的朋友們說：「祢和我們一起去嗎?」
耶穌說：「我現在不去。」
耶穌的朋友們都上了船,
從海上開往家裡去。

Walking on Water

Jesus Walks on the Sea of Galilee · Mark 6

"It is time for you to go home," Jesus said.

"Will you come with us?" His friends asked.

"Not now," said Jesus.

Jesus' friends got into their boat.

They went out on the water to go home.

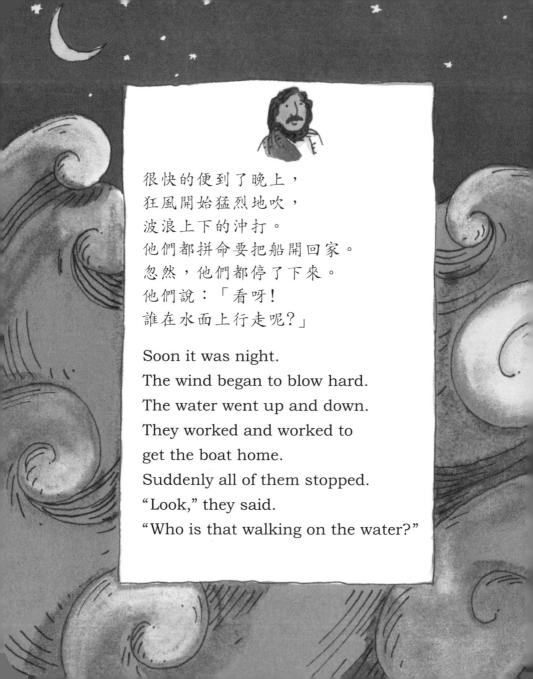

很快的便到了晚上，
狂風開始猛烈地吹，
波浪上下的沖打。
他們都拼命要把船開回家。
忽然，他們都停了下來。
他們說：「看呀！
誰在水面上行走呢？」

Soon it was night.
The wind began to blow hard.
The water went up and down.
They worked and worked to
get the boat home.
Suddenly all of them stopped.
"Look," they said.
"Who is that walking on the water?"

所有的人都很害怕。

他們說：「是一個鬼！」

走在水面上的人說：「不，我不是個鬼。」

耶穌的朋友們說：「原來是耶穌！」

他們都很高興看見了耶穌。

有些人問：「祂為甚麼能夠這樣做？」

其他的人說：「耶穌是天父的兒子，

只有天父的兒子才能夠這樣做。」

The men were afraid.

"It is a ghost!" they said.

"No, I am not a ghost,"

the Man on the water said.

"It is Jesus!" said His friends.

They were so happy that it was Jesus.

"But how can He do that?" someone asked.

"Only God's Son can do things like that,"

said others. "Jesus is God's Son."

問答題 Something to Ask

1. 你的朋友能夠在水面上行走嗎？

2. 你能夠嗎？

3. 誰曾經在水面上行走呢？

4. 祂為甚麼能夠這樣做呢？

5. 你愛天父的兒子嗎？

6. 你現在想跟祂說話嗎？

1. Can your friends walk on water?

2. Can you?

3. Who did walk on water?

4. How could He do this?

5. Do you love God's Son?

6. Will you talk to Him now?

思考題 Something to Do

這是天父創造的嗎？
Did God make this?

這些呢？
And this?

這個呢？
And this?

祂還能夠創造些甚麼？　　祂已經創造了些甚麼？

What other work can He do?

What other things did He make?

385

天父見證祂的愛子

基督變像 · 馬太福音 17

耶穌和朋友們一起來到一座很高的山。
他們越走越高、越走越高。
其中一位朋友問：
「我們為甚麼要來到這裡？」
有人說：「我們不知道，但耶穌是知道的。」
那時候，耶穌的臉開始發光，
祂的衣服也開始發光，耶穌的朋友們都很害怕。

God Talks about His Son

The Transfiguration of Christ · Matthew 17

Jesus and some friends walked up and up and up.
They went up a tall mountain.
"Why are we here?" said one friend to the other.
"We do not know," he said, "but Jesus knows."
Then Jesus' face began to shine.
His clothes began to shine, too.
Jesus' friends were so afraid.

後來，有兩個人走過來，和耶穌站在一起。
耶穌的朋友們說：「看這兩個人，
他們都是活在很久以前的人。」
這時，有一朵雲飄過來包圍著他們。
有聲音說：「這是我的愛子，
聽從祂的吩咐去做吧！」這是天父在說話。
耶穌的朋友們都很害怕，
他們都伏在耶穌的跟前。

Then two men came to be with Jesus.

"Look at those men," said Jesus' friends.

"They lived a long time ago."

Then a big cloud came over all of them.

"This is My Son," Someone said.

"Do what He says."

It was God who said this.

Jesus' friends were afraid,

so they fell down by Jesus.

他們站起來的時候，
卻再沒有看到任何人。
他們只看到耶穌。
耶穌的朋友們說：
「天父說，耶穌是祂的兒子。」
他們現在都知道，
耶穌是天父的兒子了。

When they got up,
there was no one there —
no one but Jesus.
"God said that,"
said Jesus' friends.
"God said that Jesus is His Son."
Now they knew that Jesus
was God's Son.

問答題 Something to Ask

1. 天父說了哪些關於耶穌的話?

2. 當時有誰和耶穌在一起?

3. 你怎樣才能夠討耶穌的喜悅?

4. 你快要去為耶穌做一件事嗎?

1. What did God say about Jesus?

2. Who was with Jesus then?

3. What can you do to please Jesus?

4. Will you do one thing for Jesus soon?

思考題 Something to Do

誰說耶穌是天父的兒子？

Who said that Jesus was God's Son?

耶穌自己。
Jesus did.

祂的朋友們。
So did His friends.

天父。
So did God.

你認為呢？

What do you say?

不會說感謝的人

愚蠢財主的比喻 · 路加福音 12

從前，有一個很富有的人，
他有農場、有很大的穀倉、
有很多房子、還有很多金錢。
他擁有很多的財物！
可是，他不知道怎樣去處理他所擁有的一切。
他說：「我要建造更多、更大的穀倉，
我要把穀倉建得越來越大。」

A Man Who Did Not Say Thank You

The Parable of the Rich Fool · Luke 12

There was a man who was very rich.

He had a farm. He had big barns.

He had houses. He had money.

The man had so many things!

He did not know what to do with all his things.

"I will make bigger barns," the man said.

"I will make them bigger and bigger."

這個人愛他的財物，比愛天父
還要多。他從來都沒有感謝天父
給他這一切。他從來都沒有把東西
送給別人。他說：「這些都是
我的財物，我全部都要擁有。」
天父說：「你快要死了，
你所有的東西都會給別人拿去。」

The man loved his things more than
he loved God. He did not thank God
for them. He did not give anything
away. "These are my things,"
he said. "I want them all."
But God said, "It is time for you to
die. Then others will have all
your things."

那個人不喜歡聽這些話，
但他能夠做些甚麼呢？
當天晚上，他便死了。
別人把他所有的東西都拿走了。
天父賜給我們很多美好的東西，
我們應該愛祂，
我們應該感謝祂所賜的一切！

The man did not like to hear this.
But what could he do?
That night he died.
Then others had all his things.
God gives us many good things.
We should give our love to Him.
And we should thank Him
for the things He gives to us.

問答題 Something to Ask

1. 這個人是富有還是貧窮？

2. 他願意和別人分享他的東西嗎？

3. 有甚麼事情發生在這個人身上呢？

4. 他死的時候，帶走了些甚麼？

1. Was this man rich or poor?

2. Did he want to share his things?

3. What happened to the man?

4. What things did he take with him when he died?

思考題 Something to Do

你應該怎樣向天父謝恩？
「謝謝祢賜給我美好的東西！」

How can you say thank you to God?
"Thank you for Your good things."

「我會盡力為祢去做。」
「我會把美好的東西獻給祢。」
「我會和別人分享。」
「我會告訴朋友有關祢的事。」
「我會愛祢。」

"I will do my best for You."
"I will give good things to You."
"I will share with others."
"I will tell a friend about You."
"I will love You."

401

好牧羊人

迷羊的比喻 · 路加福音 15

有一天，耶穌告訴祂的朋友們
一個迷羊的故事。
有一隻羊兒離群跑到很遠的地方。
牠迷路了，找不到回家的路。

The Good Shepherd

The Parable of the Lost Sheep · Luke 15

One day Jesus told His friends about a sheep.

It was a sheep that ran away.

The sheep went far away from the others.

It could not find the way home. It was lost!

牧羊人看著他的羊群，
發現有一隻羊兒走失了，
他很疼愛那隻羊，
他要把牠找回來。
他留下了其他的羊，
跑到離家很遠的地方，
到處尋找那隻迷路的羊兒。

The shepherd looked at his sheep.

He saw that one sheep was gone.

He loved that sheep,

and he wanted to find it.

So he left his other sheep.

He went far away from home

looking for his lost sheep.

牧羊人到處尋找他的羊兒。
他終於找到了。
牧羊人把羊兒放在他的臂膀上，
他把羊兒帶回家。
耶穌說我們好比迷路的羊兒，
我們遠離了天父；
但耶穌愛我們，祂來尋找我們。
祂幫助我們找到道路，
回到天父在天上的家。

The shepherd looked and looked
for his sheep. Then he found it.
The shepherd took the sheep into his arms.
Then he took the sheep to his home.
Jesus said that we are like the sheep.
We are far away from God.
But Jesus came to find us.
He loves us.
And He helps us find the way
to God's home in heaven.

問答題 Something to Ask

1. 那隻羊兒做了些甚麼?
   牠為甚麼會迷路?

2. 牧羊人怎樣做?

3. 我們也會像羊兒一樣嗎?

4. 耶穌怎樣幫助我們?

1. What did the sheep do?
   How did it get lost?

2. What did the shepherd do?

3. How are we like the sheep?

4. What does Jesus help us do?

思考題 Something to Do

你要怎樣做才能幫助你的家庭得到快樂呢？

How can you help your family to be happy?

耶穌和小孩子

小孩子到基督跟前來 · 馬可福音 10

耶穌的一些朋友問：「你們想做些甚麼？」
孩子們的爸爸、媽媽說：
「我們想帶孩子們來見耶穌。」
耶穌的朋友說：「你們不可以見祂。」
孩子們的爸爸、媽媽問：「為甚麼不可以？」
耶穌的朋友說：「耶穌有很多事情要做，
這就是我們的理由。」

Jesus and the Children

Children Come to Christ · Mark 10

"What do you want?"
some of Jesus' friends asked.
"We want to have our children see Jesus,"
said the mothers and fathers.
"You cannot do that," said Jesus' friends.
"Why not?" asked the mothers and fathers.
"Jesus has too many things to do,"
said His friends. "That's why."

耶穌走過來問：
「發生了甚麼事呢？」
孩子們的爸爸、媽媽說：「祢的朋友不讓
我們的孩子來見祢。」
耶穌的朋友說：「我們對他們說，
祢正忙著做別的事情。」
耶穌說：「不要讓小孩子遠離我，
他們會引領其他的人知道怎樣來親近我。」

Then Jesus came to them.
"What is the matter?" He asked.
"Your friends will not let our children see You,"
said the mothers and fathers.
Jesus' friends said, "We told them that You
were doing other things."
"Do not tell the children to stay away from Me,"
said Jesus.
"They show others how to come to Me."

耶穌讓孩子們來見祂。
祂告訴孩子們很多的事情。
祂說天父非常愛他們。
孩子們問祂:「祢也愛我們嗎?」
耶穌說:「是的,
我也要你們愛我。」

Then Jesus had the children
come to see Him.
He told them many things.
He told them how much
God loved them.
"Do You love us, too?"
the children asked.
"Yes," said Jesus.
"And I want you to love Me."

問答題 Something to Ask

1. 耶穌有沒有叫小孩子離開祂?

2. 小孩子對耶穌重要嗎?

3. 耶穌愛小孩子嗎? 你怎會知道?

4. 你怎能讓耶穌知道你愛祂?

1. Did Jesus tell the children to go away?

2. Are children important to Jesus?

3. Does Jesus love children?
   How do you know?

4. How can you show Jesus that
   you love Him?

思考題 Something to Do

耶穌喜愛圖中的哪些小孩子？

Which kinds of children does Jesus love?

一個想能夠看見的人

耶穌治好瞎子 · 路加福音 18

有一天，耶穌正在進城的時候，
遇見一個坐在路旁的窮人，
他的眼睛瞎了，不能工作。
他想找人幫助他。
當耶穌走近他時，
他對耶穌說：「幫助我！
幫助我！幫助我！幫助我！」

A Man Who Wanted to See

Jesus Heals a Blind Man · Luke 18

One day Jesus was going into a town.

A poor man sat by the road.

He wanted someone to help him.

The man could not see.

He could not work.

Then Jesus came by.

"Help me," the man said to Jesus.

"Help me! Help me! Help me!"

有些人說：「不要吵！」
可是，瞎子沒有停止叫喊。
耶穌說：「讓他到我這裡來。」
後來，有人把瞎子帶到耶穌面前。
耶穌對瞎子說：「你想要甚麼？」
瞎子說：「我想能夠看見。」
耶穌說：「好吧！你現在就可以看見。」
這樣，瞎子的眼睛馬上能夠看見了。
他是多麼的快樂啊！

"Stop that!" some people said.

But the man did not stop.

"Have him come here," said Jesus.

So some men helped bring him to Jesus.

"What do you want?" Jesus asked.

"I want to see," said the man.

"Then you will see," said Jesus.

At once the man could see.

He was so happy.

421

他現在可以看見樹木和人群。
他能夠看見耶穌。
那個人說：「謝謝祢！」
後來，他跟隨了耶穌，
幫助耶穌做祂的工作。
他很愛耶穌，
因為他知道耶穌愛他。

He could see trees.
He could see people.
And he could see Jesus.
"Thank you!" the man said.
Then the man went with Jesus
to help Him do His work.
He loved Jesus very much, and
he knew that Jesus loved him.

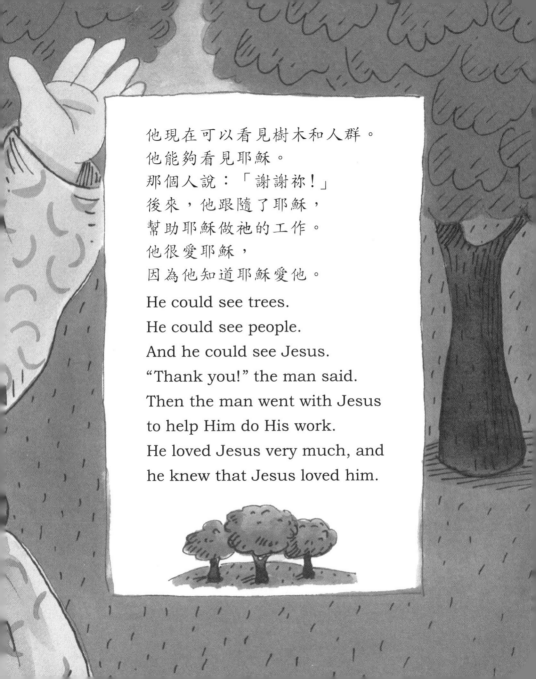

問答題 Something to Ask

1. 那個窮人想要些甚麼?

2. 耶穌為他做了些甚麼?

3. 耶穌愛窮人嗎?

4. 你怎會知道?

5. 你也愛窮人嗎?

6. 你能夠為他們做些甚麼?

1. What did the poor man want?

2. What did Jesus do for him?

3. Does Jesus love poor people?

4. How do you know?

5. Do you love poor people, too?

6. What can you do for them?

思考題 Something to Do

圖中所展示的，哪些能給你最大的幫助？
哪些能讓你感到最快樂？

Which of these will help you most?

Which will make you the most happy?

尋找新朋友

撒該和耶穌 · 路加福音 19

撒該很憂愁，他需要朋友。

可是，沒有人願意跟他做朋友。

他們都說：「撒該欺騙人，

撒該偷東西。」

有一天，撒該看見耶穌，

他說：「我想找耶穌做我的朋友。」

人們都取笑他，說：「耶穌是一位正直的人，

祂才不會跟你做朋友！」

Finding a Friend

Zacchaeus and Jesus · Luke 19

Zacchaeus was sad. He wanted friends.

But no one wanted to be his friend.

"Zacchaeus cheats," some said.

"Zacchaeus steals," said others.

One day Zacchaeus saw Jesus.

"I want Jesus to be my friend," he said.

The people laughed. "Jesus is a good Man,"
they said. "He will not be your friend."

427

無數的人包圍著耶穌。
撒該很想見耶穌，可是，他個子長得矮小，
沒法從人群當中走過去。
他說：「只要我爬上那棵大樹，
就可以看見耶穌。」
這樣，撒該便爬上了那棵大樹。
耶穌來到樹下，抬頭看見撒該。
祂說：「快下來，我要到你的家，
我要跟你做朋友。」

There were people all around Jesus.
Zacchaeus wanted to see Jesus.
But Zacchaeus was a little man.
He could not get through the crowds.
"I will climb that big tree and see Jesus," he said.
So Zacchaeus climbed the big tree.
Jesus stopped under the tree and looked up.
There was Zacchaeus.
"Come down," said Jesus. "I want to go to
your house. I want to be your friend."

撒該非常高興。
他請耶穌吃很多美味的東西。
撒該說：「我後悔曾經欺騙人。」
耶穌微笑著對他說：
「我饒恕了你。」
撒該十分高興，
他有了一個新朋友。
耶穌就是他最要好的朋友。
Zacchaeus was so happy.

He gave Jesus good things to eat.

"I'm sorry that I cheated," he said.

Jesus smiled at Zacchaeus.

"I forgive you," He said.

Zacchaeus was happy.

He had a new friend.

And Jesus is the best Friend of all.

問答題 Something to Ask

1. 撒該為甚麼沒有朋友？

2. 誰人成為了他最要好的朋友？

3. 你也想耶穌做你的朋友嗎？
   為甚麼？

1. Why did Zacchaeus has no friends?

2. Who became his best friend?

3. Would you like Jesus to be your friend?
   Why?

思考題 Something to Do

你有沒有請求耶穌做你的朋友？

你願意現在請求祂嗎？

請求耶穌饒恕你。

請求耶穌幫助你去討祂喜悅。

Have you asked Jesus to be your friend?
Would you like to do that now?
Ask Him to forgive you.
Ask Him to help you please Him.

耶穌騎驢駒

基督進入耶路撒冷 · 馬可福音 11

耶穌說：「我需要一隻驢駒，
牠可以幫助我去事奉天父。」
耶穌的朋友們到處找。
他們看看這邊、看看那邊；
可是，他們都沒有看見有驢駒。
他們問耶穌：「我們要到哪裡
才可以找到驢駒？」

認新詞   *words to know*

需要   Need
驢駒   Donkey
耶路撒冷   Jerusalem
用   Use
呼叫   Shout

Jesus on a Donkey

Christ Enters Jerusalem · Mark 11

"I need a little donkey," said Jesus.

"It will help Me do God's work."

Jesus' friends looked here. They looked there.

But they did not see a donkey.

"Where will we get a donkey?" they asked.

耶穌告訴祂的朋友們在哪裡可以找到驢駒。

祂說有人會把牠交給他們。

耶穌的朋友找到了那個人。

他們說：「我們可以用你的驢駒嗎？」

那個人說：「可以。」

那個人很高興他的驢駒能夠幫助耶穌。

耶穌騎上了驢駒，走進了一座叫耶路撒冷的大城。

很多人跟隨祂進入這座大城。

他們高聲呼叫：「耶穌是我們的王。」

Jesus told His friends where to get a donkey.

He said a man would give them one.

Jesus' friends went to the man.

"May we use your donkey?" they asked.

"Yes," said the man. He was happy

that his donkey could help Jesus.

Then Jesus got on the donkey.

He went into a big town called Jerusalem.

Many people went with Him to the big town.

They shouted, "Jesus is our King!"

耶穌在耶路撒冷告訴
人們有關天父的事。
祂告訴人們怎樣去討
天父的喜悅。祂又告訴人們，
祂將要為他們而死。天父派
耶穌到這個世界來做這件事，
這就是耶穌要替天父做的事。

In Jerusalem Jesus told people
about God.
He told them how to please God.
He told them that He would
die for them.
God had sent Jesus to do
these things.
This was the work Jesus did
for God.

問答題 Something to Ask

1. 耶穌要替天父做些甚麼工作？

2. 驢駒怎樣幫助耶穌？

3. 你能夠替天父做些甚麼工作？

1. What kind of work did Jesus do for God?

2. How did the donkey help Him?

3. What kind of work can you do for God?

思考題 Something to Do

圖中的東西如何能幫助你去事奉天父？

How can these help you do God's work?

你的
your

你的
your

你的
your

你的
your

你的
your

和耶穌共進晚餐
主耶穌的晚餐 · 馬太福音 26

耶穌的朋友們問：「我們在
哪裡吃晚餐？」
耶穌告訴他們吃晚餐的地方，
就是在耶路撒冷城的一間房子裡。
耶穌的朋友們跑到那地方去。
他們把晚餐準備好。
耶穌和祂的十二位朋友
一起在那裡吃晚餐。

Supper with Jesus
The Lord's Supper · Matthew 26

"Where will we eat?" Jesus' friends asked.

Jesus told them where it would be.

They would eat at a house in Jerusalem.

So Jesus' friends went there.

They put the supper together.

Then Jesus and His twelve friends ate together.

耶穌說：「你們吃這塊餅。
當我離開以後，你們要經常這樣做，
為的是記念我為你們而死。」
耶穌的朋友們吃了這塊餅，
心裡都很悲傷。
他們都不願意耶穌死。
耶穌又說：「你們喝這杯酒。
當我離開以後，你們要經常這樣做，
為的是記念我為你們而死。」

"Eat this bread," Jesus said. "When I am gone,
you will do this again and again.
Then you will think of the way I died for you."
Jesus' friends ate the bread.
But they were sad.
They did not want Jesus to die.
"Drink from this cup," Jesus said.
"When I am gone, you will do this
again and again. Then you will think
of the way I died for you."

耶穌的朋友們喝了這杯酒，
心裡都很悲傷，
他們都不願意耶穌死。
忽然，他們聽到有人在唱歌，
原來是耶穌。祂的朋友們也
跟著祂一起唱歌。
這是一個特別的時刻，
因為耶穌是與眾不同的。

Jesus' friends drank from the
cup. But they were sad.
They did not want Jesus to die.
Suddenly the friends heard
someone singing. It was Jesus.
Jesus' friends began to sing, too.
This was a special time because
Jesus was so special.

問答題 Something to Ask

1. 哪些人在一起吃晚餐？

2. 耶穌給祂的朋友們一些甚麼東西？
   為甚麼？

3. 誰在唱歌？

1. Who was eating together?

2. What did Jesus give His friends? Why?

3. Who was singing?

思考題 Something to Do

你在甚麼時候會想起這頓特別的晚餐？
和你的爸爸、媽媽談談這個問題吧！

When do you think of this special supper?

Talk with mother or father about this.

耶穌的大愛
基督的死 · 馬太福音 27

有人說：「把祂釘在十字架上！」

人們把耶穌釘在十字架上。

他們看著祂死去。

耶穌從來沒有傷害這些人，

可是，他們卻要傷害祂。

The Love of Jesus
The Death of Christ · Matthew 27

"Nail that Man to the cross!" someone said.

The men nailed Jesus to the cross.

Then they watched Him die.

Jesus had not hurt these men.

But they were hurting Him.

耶穌替這些人向天父禱告。
祂說：「請祢饒恕這些傷害我的人。」
這些人從來沒有見過
像耶穌一樣的人。
他們雖然傷害了耶穌，
但祂還是一樣的愛他們。
其中一個人說：「那個人是天父的兒子。」

Jesus talked to God about these men.

"Forgive them for hurting Me," He said.

These people had not seen a man like this.

They were hurting Him.

But He was loving them.

"That Man is God's Son," said one of them.

耶穌被釘死在十字架上，
是要顯明他多麼的愛這些人。
同樣地，祂也是多麼的愛你和我。
耶穌對我們的愛有多深？
祂為了愛我們而死去，
好讓我們能夠回到天父的身邊。

When Jesus died on the cross,
He showed how much He
loved them.
And He showed how much He
loves you and me.
How much does Jesus love us?
He loves us so much that He
died so we can come to God.

問答題 Something to Ask

1. 那些人為甚麼要傷害耶穌?

2. 祂有沒有傷害過那些人?

3. 祂愛那些人嗎?

4. 耶穌愛你嗎? 祂有饒恕你嗎?

5. 你也愛祂嗎?

6. 你願意告訴耶穌你愛祂嗎?

1. Why did the men hurt Jesus?

2. Did He hurt them?

3. Did He love them?

4. Does Jesus love you?
   Does He forgive you?

5. Do you love Him?

6. Would you like to tell Him this?

思考題 Something to Do

你怎樣向耶穌表示你愛祂?

你怎樣用這些不同的圖畫來表示你愛祂?

How can you show Jesus that you love Him?

How can you show it with each of these?

耶穌是活著的！

馬利亞看見復活了的基督・約翰福音 20

馬利亞非常傷心，
因為耶穌被人殺害了。
馬利亞來到安放耶穌的地方，
可是，耶穌不在那裡；
馬利亞哭著說：「有人把祂搬走了。」

Jesus Is Alive Again!

Mary Sees the Risen Christ · John 20

Mary was so sad.

Some men had killed Jesus.

Now Mary came to see where they had put Him.

But Jesus was not there.

"Someone has taken Him away," said Mary.

Mary began to cry.

這時候，有些天使向馬利亞說話。
天使問：「妳為甚麼哭泣？」
她回答說：「有人把耶穌搬走了。」
跟著，馬利亞看見有人
向著她走過來，
對她說：「妳為甚麼哭泣？」
她說：「有人把耶穌搬走了。」

Then some angels talked to Mary.
"Why are you crying?" they asked.
"Someone has taken Jesus away,"
she said.
Then Mary saw a man coming.
"Why are you crying?" He asked.
"Someone has taken Jesus away,"
she said.

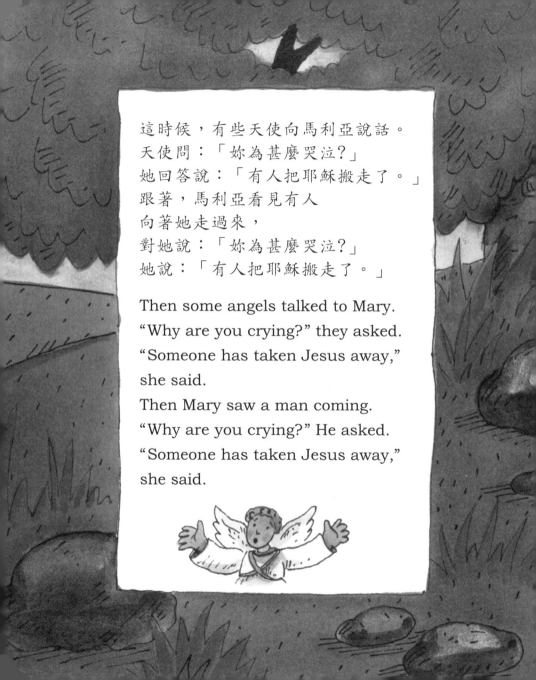

那個人說：「馬利亞！」
馬利亞說：「耶穌！」
馬利亞非常高興，
因為耶穌再次活著了！
耶穌說：「我不能和妳在一起，
我一定要回到我在天上的家。」
現在，馬利亞才知道耶穌是天父的兒子。

"Mary!" the Man said.

"Jesus!" said Mary.

Mary was so happy.

Jesus was alive again!

"I cannot stay with you," Jesus said.

"I must go back to My home in heaven."

Now Mary knew that Jesus was God's Son.

問答題 Something to Ask

1. 馬利亞為甚麼哭泣？

2. 誰來見馬利亞？

3. 祂對馬利亞說了些甚麼？

4. 誰是耶穌？

5. 馬利亞怎麼知道耶穌是天父的兒子？

1. Why did Mary cry?

2. Who came to see her?

3. What did He tell Mary?

4. Who is Jesus?

5. How did Mary know that Jesus was God's Son?

思考題 Something to Do

你怎樣知道耶穌是天父的兒子?
　　祂事奉天父。
　　祂告訴人們關於天父的事。
　　祂從來不做壞事。
　　祂幫助人從死裡再活過來。
　　祂說祂是天父的兒子。
　　祂被殺死後再活過來。

How do you know that Jesus is God's Son?
　　He did God's work.
　　He told others about God.
　　He did not do bad things.
　　He helped some people come
　　alive after they died.
　　He said that He was God's Son.
　　He came alive after some men killed Him.

向眾人傳揚耶穌

天父的家興旺 · 使徒行傳 1-8

耶穌說：「到世界各地去，
告訴人們有關我為他們所做的事。」
耶穌講完了這些話，
便回到天上的家去了。

Telling Others about Jesus

The Church Grows · Acts 1-8

"Go to all the world," Jesus said.
"Tell people everywhere
about what I did for them."
After Jesus said these things
He went back to heaven to stay.

耶穌的朋友們都知道祂是
天父的兒子，祂為他們而死。
祂復活後曾經和他們生活在一起。
只有天父的兒子才能夠這樣做。
他們知道耶穌怎樣帶領
人們去認識天父。
他們走到人們那裡去、
告訴人們關於耶穌的事。

Jesus' friends knew that He was God's Son.
He had died for them.
Then He had come back to live with them.
Only God's Son could do that!
They knew that Jesus showed people
the way to know God.
So they went to all the people.
They went to tell them about Jesus.

469

他們說：「耶穌愛你們，
祂要幫助你們去認識天父。」
有些人聽到了很高興，
可是，有些人說：「走開吧！」
耶穌的朋友們看見那些愛耶穌
的人，都很高興。

"Jesus loves you," they said.
"He wants to help you get to
know God." Some people liked
what they heard.
But others said, "Go away!"
Jesus' friends were happy when
some people did come to
love Jesus.

問答題 Something to Ask

1. 耶穌要祂的朋友們做些甚麼?

2. 他們需要怎樣做?

3. 他們為甚麼要這樣做?

4. 祂要你為祂做些甚麼?

5. 你會怎樣告訴別人有關耶穌的事?

1. What did Jesus ask His friends to do?

2. How did they do it?

3. Why did they do it?

4. What does He want you to do for Him?

5. How can you tell others about Him?

思考題 Something to Do

你應該在甚麼地方告訴別人關於耶穌的事？

在你的家？
At your house?

在朋友的家？
At a friend's house?

Where should you tell others about Jesus?

在這裡，在那裡，
在任何地方？
Here and there
and everywhere?

認新詞　　words to know

離開　Leave
腓利　Philip

一個聽到耶穌的人

腓利和埃提阿伯太監 · 使徒行傳 8

有一位天使對腓利說：
「離開這個城鎮，到我吩咐
你要去的地方。」
這樣，腓利便離開那個城鎮，
走了很遠的路，
來到天使吩咐他去的地方。
腓利說：「這裡一個人也沒有，
我怎能替天父工作呢？」

A Man Hears about Jesus

Philip and the Ethiopian · Acts 8

"Leave this town," an angel told Philip.

"Go where I tell you to go."

Philip left that town.

He went far away to the place

where the angel told him to go.

"But there are no people here," said Philip.

"How can I do God's work here?"

475

後來，腓利看見有人走過來；
那人正在看著記載天父話語的書。
腓利問他：「你看得明白嗎？」
那個人說：「不明白，我需要別人
幫助，你願意幫助我嗎？」
腓利說：「好！我願意，
是天父派我來幫助你的。」

Then Philip saw a man coming.
The man was looking at God's
Word. "Do you know what it
says?" Philip asked.
"No," said the man. "I need
someone to help me.
Will you help me?"
"Yes," said Philip, "I will."
"God sent me here to help you."

這樣，腓利把天父的話告訴了那個人，
他還把耶穌的事告訴他。
那人對腓利說：「我要照著耶穌的吩咐去做。」
腓利聽了很高興。
他現在才知道天父為甚麼要派
他到那個地方去。
他知道那個人會把關於耶穌的事
去告訴更多的人。

So Philip told the man
what God's Word said.
He told the man about Jesus.
"I want to do what Jesus says,"
the man told Philip.
Philip was so happy.
Now he knew why God had sent him there.
He knew that this man
would tell many others about Jesus.

問答題 Something to Ask

1. 那人要求腓利幫助他做些甚麼?

2. 他為甚麼需要別人的幫助
   去認識聖經?

3. 你能幫助誰? 你能幫助他們
   做些甚麼?

4. 你要怎樣做才能明白更多聖經上的真理?

1. What did the man want Philip to help him do?

2. Why do you want others to help you know God's Word?

3. Who can you help? What can you do to help them?

4. What can you do to know more about God's Word?

思考題 Something to Do

你從哪裡聽到有關耶穌的事？

Where do you hear about Jesus?

聖經？
God's Word?

有關耶穌的書？
Books about Jesus?

爸爸和媽媽？
Mother
and father?

天父的家？
God's house?

愛耶穌的朋友？
Friends who
love Jesus?

比太陽更光亮

掃羅歸主 · 使徒行傳 9

掃羅憎恨耶穌。

他也憎恨耶穌的朋友。

他不願意看見有人跟隨耶穌。

掃羅不相信耶穌是天父的兒子，

他認為耶穌已經死了。

他說：「人們為甚麼要跟隨

一個已經死去的人？」

掃羅設法去傷害耶穌的朋友們。

Brighter than the Sun

Saul's Conversion · Acts 9

Saul hated Jesus.

And he hated Jesus' friends.

He did not want people to follow Jesus.

Saul did not think that Jesus was God's Son.

Saul thought Jesus was dead. He said,

"Why should people follow a dead person?"

So Saul tried to hurt Jesus' friends.

有一天，掃羅要去大馬色城，
他要去傷害耶穌的朋友。
在路上的時候，
有一件事發生了：天空忽然發出
強烈的光，比太陽還要光亮。
強烈的光叫掃羅跌倒在地上。

One day Saul went to a city
called Damascus.
He went to hurt Jesus' friends.
But on the way, something
happened.
Suddenly the sky was bright.
It was brighter than the sun.
It was so bright that Saul fell
down.

接著，有聲音從天上對他說：
「不要再逼迫我。」
掃羅問：「祢是誰？祢要我做些甚麼？」
他非常害怕，因為從來沒有人
會從天上對他說話。
天上的聲音說：「我是耶穌，你來跟隨我！」
現在，掃羅知道耶穌是活著的。
他知道耶穌是天父的兒子；祂住在天堂裡。
他願意永永遠遠都跟隨耶穌。

Then Someone from heaven said, "Stop hurting Me."
"Who are You?" Saul asked.
"What do You want me to do?"
He was afraid. No one from heaven
had talked to him before.
"I am Jesus," the Person said. "Follow Me!"
Now Saul knew that Jesus was alive.
He knew that Jesus was God's Son.
He knew that Jesus was in heaven.
He would follow Jesus as long as he lived.

問答題 Something to Ask

1. 掃羅為甚麼憎恨耶穌的朋友們?

2. 他要他們做些甚麼?

3. 他為甚麼要到大馬色城?

4. 誰跟他說話? 耶穌說了些甚麼?

5. 掃羅為甚麼跟隨了耶穌?

1. Why did Saul hate Jesus' friends?

2. What did he want them to do?

3. Why did he go to Damascus?

4. Who talked to him?
   What did Jesus say?

5. Why did Saul become Jesus' follower?

思考題 Something to Do

你有沒有對耶穌說：

「祢想我替祢做些甚麼？」

你願意現在就問祂嗎？

Have you asked Jesus,

"What would You like me to do for You?"

 Would you like to ask Him now?

認新詞 | words to know
保羅 | Paul
西拉 | Silas
震動 | Shake
門 | Door

在監獄裡高歌

保羅和西拉在監獄 · 使徒行傳 16

保羅和西拉都事奉天父；

他們告訴人們耶穌就是天父的兒子；

他們幫助人們去愛耶穌。

可是，有些人不喜歡這樣做。

他們憎恨耶穌和祂的朋友們。

他們高聲叫喊：

「把這些做壞事的人，

都關進監獄裡去！」

Singing in Jail

Paul and Silas in Prison · Acts 16

Paul and Silas were doing God's work.

They were telling people that Jesus is God's Son.

They were helping people love Jesus.

But some men did not like that.

They hated Jesus. They hated Jesus' friends, too.

"Put those men in jail!" they shouted.

"They are doing bad things."

保羅和西拉都被關進監獄裡。
當天晚上，保羅和西拉唱歌
讚美天父的時候，
整座監獄忽然震動起來，
監獄門都打開了。
看守監獄的人非常害怕。
如果保羅和西拉逃走了，
他會被人傷害，所以他想自殺。

Some men put Paul and Silas in
jail. That night Paul and Silas
began to sing songs about God.
Suddenly the jail began to shake.
The door of the jail broke.
The man at the jail was afraid
that someone would hurt him
if Paul and Silas got away.
So he tried to kill himself.

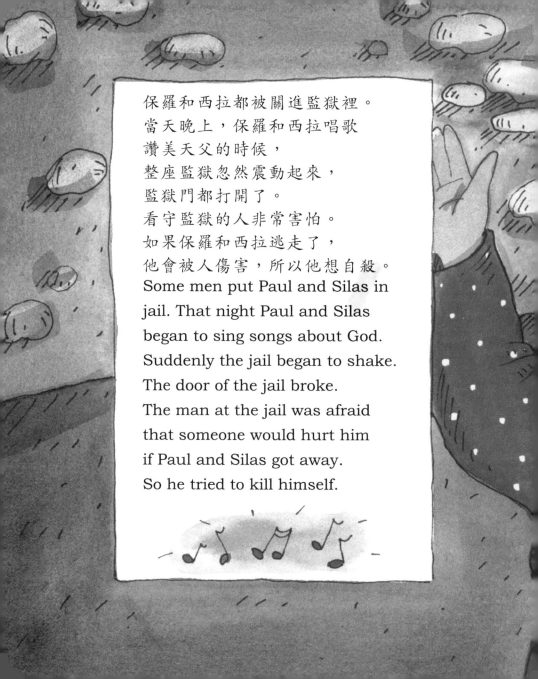

保羅對他說：「不要傷害自己，
我們都在這裡。」
現在，看守的人知道是天父保守保羅和西拉。
他說：「我請求耶穌饒恕我，
我要愛祂和跟隨祂。我應該怎樣做呢？」
保羅說：「求耶穌饒恕你吧！」
看守的人聽從了，他向耶穌禱告。
他的家人都做了耶穌的朋友，全家都很快樂。
你想他們也會快樂地唱歌嗎？

"Stop," said Paul. "We are all here."
Now the man knew that God took care
of Paul and Silas.
"I want Jesus to forgive me," he said.
"I want to love Jesus and follow Him.
What should I do?"
"Ask Jesus to forgive you," said Paul.
So the man did. He prayed to Jesus.
His family became Jesus' friends, too.
They were all happy.
Do you think they sang happy songs, too?

問答題 Something to Ask

1. 人們為甚麼把保羅和西拉
   關進監獄裡?

2. 他們在監獄裡做了些甚麼?

3. 當你受到傷害的時候,你會唱歌,
   或是說些難聽的話?

4. 有甚麼恩典落在那看守
   監獄的人身上?

1. Why did men put Paul and
   Silas in jail?

2. What did they do in jail?

3. What do you do when you get hurt?
   Do you sing, or do you say bad things?

4. What good thing happened to the
   man at the jail?

思考題 Something to Do

我們在甚麼時候會唱歌讚美天父？
When should we sing songs about God?

當事情順利的時候？	When things go well?
當別人傷害我的時候？	When people hurt me?
當別人幫助我的時候？	When people help me?
當我快樂的時候？	When I am happy?
當我不快樂的時候？	When I am not happy?

保羅是勇敢的助手

保羅的船遇難 · 使徒行傳 27

人們大聲呼叫:「我們可以做些甚麼?」
保羅乘坐的船遇到了大風暴;
狂風把他們的船吹得東搖西擺;
大雨不停的掉下來。
船上的人說:「我們很快就會被淹死!」
他們實在是沒有甚麼可以做的。

Paul Is a
Brave Helper

Paul's Shipwreck · Acts 27

"What can we do?" the people cried.

The wind made their boat go here and there.

The rain came down on them.

They were in a bad storm.

There was nothing they could do.

"We will all be killed!" they said.

保羅說：「不要怕，天父告訴我，
所有的人都不會被淹死。」
跟著，保羅告訴他們關於天父的
事，他說天父會幫助他們。
保羅非常勇敢，
他知道天父和他們在一起。

"No," said Paul, "God told me
that no one will be killed."
Then Paul told them about
God. He told them how God
would help them.
Paul was very brave.
He knew that God was
with them.

502

大風暴終於把船弄沉了。
船上的人卻沒有和船一起沉下去。
天父幫助他們上了岸。
船上的人很高興保羅跟他們在一起。
他們很高興保羅是天父
勇敢的助手。

The storm made the boat
sink under the water.
But the people did not go down with it.
God helped them get to the land.
Then the people were happy that
Paul was with them.
They were happy that he was
God's brave helper.

問答題 Something to Ask

1. 大風暴的時候，保羅做了些甚麼？

2. 當其他人感到害怕的時候，
   保羅怎樣表現出他的勇氣？

3. 這件事和替天父工作有甚麼關係？

4. 當別人感到害怕的時候，
   你該怎樣做才能表現你的勇氣？

1. What did Paul do when a storm came?

2. How was he brave when others
   were afraid?

3. How was this doing God's work?

4. How can you be brave when others
   are afraid?

思考題 Something to Do

圖中的人怎樣去幫助那些受驚的人？

How are these people helping others who are afraid?

幫助朋友

保羅和阿尼西母・腓利門書

阿尼西母逃走了！
阿尼西母是腓利門的僕人。
他偷了腓利門的東西，
所以他要逃走，
離開腓利門的家。
阿尼西母逃到一個大城去。

Helping a Friend

Paul and Onesimus・Philemon

Onesimus had run away.

Onesimus had worked for Philemon.

But he had run away from Philemon.

Onesimus had taken some
of Philemon's things, too.

Onesimus ran away to a big town.

保羅在城中遇見阿尼西母。
保羅告訴他有關耶穌的事。
阿尼西母聽完了，開始有了
愛耶穌的心。
他想回到腓利門的家；
他想要求腓利門再收留他。
他希望腓利門愛他，不要傷害他。

Paul saw Onesimus in the big
town. He told him about Jesus.
Onesimus began to love Jesus.
Then he wanted to go back
home to Philemon.
He wanted Philemon to take
him back. He wanted Philemon
to love him and not hurt him.

保羅替阿尼西母寫了一封信給腓利門。
保羅的信上說：「腓利門，
阿尼西母現在是一個愛
耶穌的人，他要做正直的事，
請你再收留他做你的僕人吧！」
阿尼西母很高興找到像保羅的朋友；
他很高興保羅幫助他去
做正直的事。

So Paul wrote to Philemon for Onesimus.
"Philemon," Paul said,
"Onesimus loves Jesus now.
He wants to do what is right.
Will you take him back to work for you?"
Onesimus was happy to have a friend like Paul.
He was happy that Paul helped him do
what was right.

問答題 Something to Ask

1. 阿尼西母做了些甚麼事？

2. 他為甚麼要回到腓利門的家？

3. 保羅怎樣幫助阿尼西母？

4. 你猜腓利門會怎樣做？

5. 你會怎樣去幫助別人
   替天父工作？

1. What did Onesimus do?

2. Why did he want to go back
   to Philemon?

3. How did Paul help Onesimus?

4. What do you think Philemon did?

5. How can you help others do what
   they should for God?

思考題 Something to Do

你會怎樣幫助朋友去做正直的事？

How can you help a friend do what is right?

跟他說話？	Talk to him?
作弄他？	Make fun of him?
跟他一起工作？	Work with him?
求天父幫助他？	Ask God to help him?
對別人說他的壞話？	Tell others bad things about him?

513

目　錄

515

518

Story List